THE DOG WITH GOLDEN EYES

The Dog with Golden Eyes

FRANCES WILBUR

MARK COYLE, *Illustrator*

MILKWEED EDITIONS

© 1998, Text by Frances Wilbur
© 1998, Illustrations by Mark Coyle
All rights reserved. Except for brief quotations in critical articles or reviews, no part of this book may be reproduced in any manner without prior written permission from the publisher: Milkweed Editions, 430 First Avenue North, Suite 400, Minneapolis, MN 55401
Distributed by Publishers Group West

Published 1998 by Milkweed Editions
Printed in the United States of America
Cover design by Gail Wallinga
Cover and interior illustrations by Mark Coyle
Interior design by Will Powers
The text of this book is set in Amerigo BT.
        00 01 02 5 4 3 2
First Edition

Milkweed Editions is a not-for-profit publisher. We gratefully acknowledge support from the Alliance for Reading Funders: Cray Research, a Silicon Graphics Company, Dayton Hudson Circle of Giving; Ecolab Foundation; Jay and Rose Phillips Foundation; Rathmann Family Foudation; Target Stores; and United Arts School and Partnership Funds.
        Other support has been provided by Elmer L. and Eleanor J. Andersen Foundation; James Ford Bell Foundation; Dayton's, Mervyn's, and Target Stores by the Dayton Hudson Foundation; Doherty, Rumble & Butler Foundation; Dorsey and Whitney Foundation; General Mills Foundation; Honeywell Foundation; Hubbard Foundation; Jerome Foundation; McKnight Foundation; Minnesota State Arts Board through an appropriation by the Minnesota State Legislature; Challenge and Creation and Presentation Programs of the National Endowment for the Arts; Norwest Foundation on behalf of Norwest Bank Minnesota, Norwest Investment Management & Trust, Lowry Hill, Norwest Investment Services, Inc.; Lawrence and Elizabeth Ann O'Shaughnessy Charitable Income Trust in honor of Lawrence M. O'Shaughnessy; Oswald Family Foundation; Piper Jaffray Companies, Inc.; Ritz Foundation on behalf of Mr. and Mrs. E. J. Phelps Jr.; John and Beverly Rollwagen Fund of the Minneapolis Foundation; St. Paul Companies, Inc.; Star Tribune/Cowles Media Foundation; James R. Thorpe Foundation; and by the support of generous individuals.

Library of Congress Cataloging-in-Publication Data

Wilbur, Frances.
        The dog with golden eyes / Frances Wilbur. — 1st ed.
            p. cm.
        Summary: Lonely thirteen-year-old Cassie commences her journey into adulthood when she unwittingly befriends an arctic wolf lost in her town and decides to care for him until she can find his real owners.
        ISBN 1-57131-614-0 (cl). — ISBN 1-57131-615-9 (pb)
        [1. Wolves—Fiction.   2. Wildlife rescue—Fiction.]   I. Title.
PZ7.W64115Do   1998
[Fic]—dc21
                                                        97-43266
                                                           CIP
                                                            AC

For Tundra,
whose eyes were golden,
and for Sandy,
who opened my eyes

THE DOG WITH GOLDEN EYES

CHAPTER
1

"One more bite," Cassandra said out loud. "Just one more bite, and then I'll go inside."

She sat all by herself on the top step of their creaky wooden back porch. Jars of syrup and marshmallow creme and boxes of cookies and crackers surrounded her on the steps. This is a great scientific experiment, she thought. Who else could think of this? She'd figure out exactly how to get the very best, most delicious-tasting snack ever.

Carefully balanced on her slightly pudgy lap was a package of chocolate chips. She reached down for a box of sugar cookies. She frowned. Sugar cookies had been Lindsay's favorite—Lindsay, her former, very ex–best friend. She and Lindsay used to do everything together, from being lab partners in science to shopping to even crank calling guys. But that was before Lindsay found Shannon and Joanna.

Cassie tightened her mouth. Someday, Lindsay would be sorry. Someday, Lindsay would come back on her hands and knees, begging to be best friends again. "No way!" Cassie would snap at her.

Cassie opened the box of sugar cookies. She took

one out. Why is it suddenly so quiet? she wondered. Even the birds had stopped singing.

Something felt weird. Was—was something watching her? Cassie looked across at the row of liquidambar trees that marked the boundary of her yard. Behind the trees, the ground began rising from a gentle slope to a hill. The hill was dotted with silvery green spikes of yucca and clumps of dark juniper and oaks. But no one was there. She shut her eyes and listened. Silence. The feeling of being watched didn't disappear. Slowly, she opened her eyes.

Straight ahead of her, sitting on his haunches beside one of the liquidambar trees, was the most beautiful white dog she had ever seen. He seemed to be looking at something far away, yet she was certain he was really watching her. She let out her breath.

No wind ruffled the long white fur, but the sun shone through the edges of the pricked white ears and across the top of his head so he looked as if he wore a halo. His front legs were very long and thin. A heavy white ruff of fur covered his chest, and a thick white brush of tail rested on the ground beside his haunches. His pointed silver muzzle ended in a very black nose.

A dog! she breathed. Maybe he was lost! If only she could have him. Animals—especially dogs—were better than a lot of people, most people, in fact. Maybe she could make friends with him. Her first instinct was to rush forward and pet him, but at the same moment, a feeling of awe and respect swept over her. If ever a dog were a king, this dog was one.

She wanted to say, "Oh, let me be your friend," but she was silent. He sat still as a statue, looking off into the distance. Cassie began to wonder if he were a vision of some sort. Perhaps he wasn't even real. Maybe she was imagining him. She closed her eyes, counted to ten, and opened them.

There was nothing by the tree.

She gasped, angry and disappointed. How could he have seemed so real? She scowled, and then the part of her mind that was more scientific took command. Down the steps she went and crossed the straggly lawn to where she thought she had seen the animal. She examined the ground. Sure enough, there were paw prints, enormous ones. She looked all around.

She could see nothing unusual on the hillside or among the shadows of the trees. After a while, she went back to the steps and took out another sugar cookie. Carefully spreading it with peanut butter, she put a second cookie on top and walked back to the liquidambar. She put the peanut butter and cookie sandwich on the ground where the dog had been and returned to the steps.

If only the dog would come back! She sat down and waited. How she'd love to be able to tell her dad about the white dog. He loved animals, too. She sighed. She really missed him.

What hurt so much was that he hadn't even said good-bye to Cassie. She and her dad had gotten along great together. It was her mom who was a pain. No matter what Cassie did, or how hard she tried, it seemed like her mom was never satisfied. If she got a B+ on a paper, her mom wanted to know why it wasn't an A.

Cassie looked back at the liquidambar tree. There was still no dog. Her gaze went beyond the line of trees. The sloping brown California hills were just beginning to turn green from the first autumn rains. The sunlight shone through the leaves of the liquidambars. They looked as though they were on fire.

She could finish her taste experiment now, she remembered. But if she looked down, she might miss the white dog. She sat still and watched.

The sunlight ended abruptly, the hill turned black against the evening sky, and the fiery leaves of the liquidambars became ordinary pieces of colored paper. Several stars winked in the sky, and Cassie felt a cool wind rising from the canyon. She shook her head, gathered up the remains of her experiment, and went inside.

Why hadn't the dog come back? She could try to be its friend. Maybe she could even keep it. She had always wanted a dog. But whenever Cassie brought it up, her mom always said no.

"I don't want any animals around," her mother would say in her don't-argue-with-me-now voice. "No. Absolutely not. I don't want any animal around that has to be fed and looked after. We are *not* going to have a dog."

Once, her mother had even brought up the subject herself. "You bring home a dog, I'll call the dog catcher, and the dog will go to the pound. And you know what happens next."

Unfortunately Cassie did. She bit her lip and instantly tried to shut out of her mind the memory of the trip to the pound that her science class had taken. She didn't want to remember the rows of whining, wiggling, tail-wagging dogs in the little cages, eyes shining with hope that the next visitor might take them home. Cassie gritted her teeth in an effort to forget about the countdown to the last day of possible adoption. She knew that if there was no adoption, no one to pay for the license, there would be only a short countdown to the day that dog had to be put to sleep.

Her science teacher had planned the field trip so the class would understand how important it was to have a pet fixed to keep it from having little ones. There were too many unwanted animals. Cassie had wanted to adopt them all, but she couldn't adopt even one.

But if the white dog came back, maybe he would adopt *her*. Her mom wouldn't have to know, would she? Tomorrow she would look through the refrigerator to see what she could give him. Oh, how she wanted him to return!

CHAPTER
2

Cassie settled herself in front of the television with a big bag of corn chips. Her favorite program came right after the news. She put up with reports of freeway smashups and gang violence in order to watch the TV show about a teenage girl and her friends. They looked like they were having a great time. Cassie sighed.

Cassie remembered when she and Lindsay used to take turns calling each other after supper and talk for an hour or so. Then one evening Lindsay's mother had answered the phone and said Lindsay wasn't there.

"She's gone to the mall with Shannon and Joanna."

Cassie's hand was shaking as she put down the receiver.

"How could Lindsay do this to me?"

Her brain was numb.

She waited all evening for a call from Lindsay with some sort of an explanation, but the phone never rang.

The next day when they passed each other in the hall between classes, Lindsay stopped and said quickly to Cassie, "Sorry I wasn't home when you called. I had to go shopping."

That was all!

A couple of days later Lindsay did phone her, but everything was different. They had talked only ten minutes.

And now Lindsay only smiled and nodded to her when they passed in the hallway. Sometimes when they passed each other, Lindsay didn't even see Cassie. She would be busy talking with Shannon and Joanna. The three girls seemed to go everywhere together, linked arm in arm, talking and laughing.

I don't care, Cassie told herself. She was determined not to care. She thought about the white dog.

The news came on the television screen. The lead story was about heavy rains and flooding in another county. People had been marooned, houses and bridges washed away. Ordinarily such tragedies would have fascinated Cassie, and she would have watched for the rescue of animals by their owners, but the screen was a blur. In her mind she saw only the white dog with the halo of sunlight. She didn't notice that her favorite show had begun—in her head she was romping in the backyard with the white dog. Neither did she hear the front door open and close.

"Hi, I'm home," announced her mother's tired voice.

Cassie came back to the present and looked up. "Hi, Mom," she said carefully. She held out the sack of corn chips to her mother.

Her mother shook her head, sank into the brown upholstered chair, and leaned back with her eyes shut. Her waitress uniform was spotted, and strands of brown hair had escaped from beneath the little cap that was supposed to be perky but wasn't. Her face wore a strained expression that made her look older than usual.

"I don't suppose there's any mail," said her mother.

"Sort of," said Cassie. "Some bills, a bunch of ads, and a catalog of car parts."

"I meant mail from your father. I was hoping there'd be a check."

"No," said Cassie shortly. She hated to be reminded of her father leaving home. She knew her parents weren't divorced, but her father sent a check once in a while to help out. It was really a money order, not a check, and the postmark on the envelope was always San Francisco. Her father was a car mechanic and a really good one. Cassie tried to figure out where he might be, but the San Francisco phone book had pages and pages of garages where her father might have gone to work.

Before he left, he had his business at home and worked on cars in their own garage. Lots of people brought him their cars instead of taking them to a regular garage because he was so good and didn't charge as much. Cassie had loved watching him work. She knew he liked having her there because he always explained to her what he was doing and why. He showed her how to start with the problem and

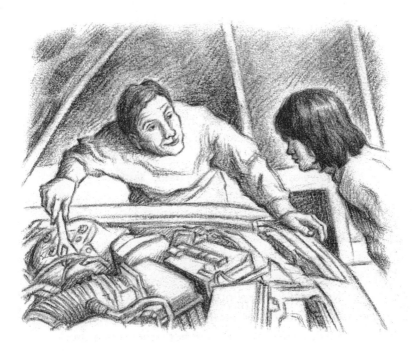

step-by-step eliminate the possible causes. "Always start with the simplest thing first," he told her. It was fun watching him figure out how to fix a problem. She always had a good time with her father.

She remembered the time her father had taken her to the circus. Her mother didn't want to go with them. "It's so dusty, and it smells of animals," she said.

Her father bought them two giant cones of pink cotton candy. They ate them, laughing and talking, walking up and down the aisles between the cages of animals waiting to perform. She sighed. How she missed him.

Cassie's mother sat up and opened her eyes. "I saw something funny as I drove home," she said. "It was a white truck that read 'County Animal Control' on the side. My headlights picked it out. That must be a fancy name for dog catcher. I haven't seen any dogs running loose around here, have you?"

Cassie gulped and said, "Everybody around here I know of always keeps their dogs on a leash." She quickly asked her mother, "Did you eat at work?"

"No. It's hard to eat after looking at food all day. And listening to everybody's problems." She sighed. "I'm really not hungry, but you can fix me something."

Her mother worked at the Red Baron Burger fast-food place a couple of miles from their house. Cassie couldn't understand why the people her mother worked with always told her their problems. Her mother wasn't the kind of person Cassie could tell *her* problems to.

Cassie went into the kitchen. There was plenty of ground beef—enough for their tortillas as well as for the white dog. She put half of the ground beef away in the back of the refrigerator for the white dog. She cooked the rest of the meat and made four tortillas, putting two on each plate.

She chopped lettuce and tomatoes and heaped them over the ground beef, shook out the contents of a package of crumbled yellow cheese on top of the tomatoes, and liberally splashed taco sauce from a jar over the small mountain of food on each plate.

"Supper's ready, Mom," announced Cassie, putting the plates on the kitchen table and hastily assembling forks and spoons and paper towels for napkins. "Mom?"

Her mother appeared in the doorway. "Whew! That's way too much food. It looks good, but you always cook too much."

"Maybe not, Mom," said Cassie. She wished her mother didn't always follow a compliment with "but." "I'll eat what you don't want."

"I know," said her mother. She looked at Cassie. "You're getting . . ." She stopped abruptly, and a smile wavered across her face. "You look nice in that blouse. That color's good on you."

"Thanks Mom." Cassie decided that the school counselor's last conference with her mother had helped a little bit.

Earlier this year, Cassie had decided to quit studying because she could never please her mother. There was no point in even trying. Then after the last report card, when her grade in science was an A and the rest of her grades were pretty bad, her mother told Cassie that the principal had asked her to go to school to meet with the counselor.

When her mother came home after the meeting, Cassie had asked, "What did the counselor say?"

Her mother had hesitated. "He said you were an underachiever."

"What does that mean?"

"It means you have an awful lot of ability. I told him I knew that. Then he said I should let you work at your own speed and not say things to discourage you."

Well, Cassie had thought, I hope she takes his advice.

They sat down at the table and Cassie attacked the food. She ate quickly. From time to time she glanced at her mother's plate. At last her mother put down her fork.

"Are you through, Mom?" asked Cassie, and after a pause followed by a nod from her mother, she deftly whisked the food from her mother's plate onto her own. "I'll bet you're glad we never waste any food."

"Sure," said her mother. She stood up. "I'm really beat. I'm going to bed. Don't forget to turn off the TV."

Cassie was startled. She didn't even remember turning it on. She looked down at the dishes with a little frown. When she had rinsed the dishes and put them in the dishwasher, she took the rest of the corn chips from the living room, turned off the TV, and went to her room.

From her bookshelves she pulled her well-worn copy of the *Complete Dog Book*, published by the American Kennel Club. She stretched out on her bed and turned the pages. Cassie was sure she had never seen a dog quite like that white dog. She had seen him for less than a minute, and she couldn't find a picture that looked like him. After a while, she closed the book, put the empty corn-chip sack in the bag marked "paper only," and went quietly out the back door.

She sat down on the top step and stared into the darkness. There was no moon, but the low clouds glowed pink with the reflected neon lights of Los Angeles. She saw dimly the pale mark of the cookie sandwich she had left beside the tree. For nearly half an hour, she kept vigil without moving while her mind sent a message to the white dog. "Come back to me. I won't let the dog catcher get you." There was only the wind in the trees, an occasional call of some night bird, and the crickets singing in their high, thin voices.

Cassie shivered and finally went inside to bed. She remembered her mother seeing the dog-catcher truck. Cassie would have to make friends quickly with the dog, before he was caught and taken to the pound. Tomorrow she would take the ground beef she had saved and put it outside by the liquidambar tree.

CHAPTER
3

The buzz of the alarm clock woke Cassie. She turned it off and groaned at the thought of another school day. Then she remembered the white dog. Quickly she dressed and went outside to the liquidambar trees. The cookie sandwich was gone.

Cassie studied the ground carefully. Not a crumb remained, but there were new paw prints, big ones. Other dogs in the neighborhood could have eaten the sandwich, but because of the size of the paw prints, she was sure it was the white dog. She smiled all through two bowls of Wheaties. She remembered the ground beef she had saved from supper. This afternoon after school, she would feed him. Her mother was still asleep.

As she left the house, she saw Shannon and Joanna walking to school ahead of her. If only Cassie's mother had given her a romantic name like Shannon or Joanna. They not only had beautiful names, but they wore beautiful clothes, the newest things, which the other girls quickly copied. No wonder Lindsay had left Cassie to hang out with them.

Shannon and Joanna had to walk past Cassie's house every day on the way to school, but they never asked Cassie to join them. Several times she had seen them look at her and giggle. She could tell they were making fun of her. Cassie hated them. She always hurried out before they came or hung back so they wouldn't meet. Today she walked slowly behind them, wishing she had someone she could walk with and talk about the white dog. She wished she could tell Lindsay about him. Lindsay loved animals almost as much as Cassie did.

She plodded toward school and kept her head down as she walked.

Cassie did not like school for two very good reasons. The first was that in a lot of classes, from time to time each student had to give an oral report. Even if she knew the subject well, when she got up in front of the class and saw the rows of unfriendly faces, her mouth went dry, and her tongue stuck to the roof of her mouth. When she could talk, her voice came out in a squeak, and all the students laughed. Then they stared at her all during her speech.

The second reason was that everything except science was an absolute waste. In her English class, they were studying poetry, which she hated because the teacher never let a poem alone. He picked it all to pieces until there wasn't anything left to wonder about.

For math, the class had only four computers. The students were supposed to take turns, but somehow Cassie hardly ever got her chance. She longed to be able to use a computer, but she had to sit in silence, watching the other students as their fingers poked the keys and blue type appeared like magic on the screen.

In French, the teacher was a real nerd. In social studies, they forged the Constitution week after week, and it was *boring,* BORING. P.E. was unspeakable torture. Only in science class did Cassie feel that her attention was worthwhile.

The science room smelled strongly of small animals. Around the room in cages lived numerous rabbits, six hamsters, some chameleons, a family of African lizards, two iguanas, and four spotted guinea pigs. Most of the kids complained about the smell, but each time Cassie walked into the science room, she took a deep breath and felt almost at peace with the world.

Her lab partner, Joe Pinatelli, was just the opposite. He hated the smell. He always came into the room holding his nose and making a face. When he couldn't hold his breath any longer, he would let it out with a noise like steam escaping from a tea-kettle. The girls would laugh as though he had done something clever.

Joe was always laughing or smiling, showing white, straight teeth. His black hair hung in curls over his smooth forehead. He wore tee shirts printed with volleyball and surfing logos, and he was good in sports even though he wasn't very tall. He was one of the best players on the A soccer team.

Joe stood in the doorway, gasped, pretended to almost fall, and held his nose. He staggered past a group of girls and reached his desk. When he was sure they were watching, he blew out his breath and rolled his eyes. They laughed. He turned to Cassie.

"Sick," he said. "It's still my turn to take care of all those stinkin' hamsters."

Cassie wanted to say, "They don't stink. If you cleaned their cages like you should, they wouldn't smell at all," but she didn't say anything. Usually Joe turned the things she said into a joke. She had learned to keep her mouth shut.

Joe said, "Those hamsters prob'ly smell pretty good to other hamsters, don't you think?"

Cassie felt her face turn pink. She began studying the textbook. She hated being Joe's lab partner almost as much as she was sure Joe hated being hers, but the teacher had assigned them and refused to make a change. Cassie wouldn't have minded so much except that Joe never took anything seriously, not even science, and especially not the science teacher, Mr. Crowell. Still, having Joe as a lab partner was better than having someone like that awful Brad Keeler, who not only didn't like animals, but who went hunting with his dad and bragged about how many animals and birds he had killed.

She remembered the first day he had come to their school. He was tall and had straight blond hair that he combed back in a sort of wave, and he looked very athletic. The girls went crazy over him, but when one of the boys asked him if he was going out for football, he said, "Naaah, I don't have time for that. I got my hunting license, and my dad and I go hunting every weekend during the season. Last year I got me a deer, my first one. This year we're going up to Bishop in the mountains. That's where the best hunting is."

Cassie shuddered every time she thought about him.

The kids made fun of the science teacher because he was very short and peered through his horn-rimmed glasses as though he were trying to see through fog. His name, Mr. Crowell, rhymed with bowl. He was fidgety, too, never standing still. While he talked to the class, he usually rocked forward on his toes, then back onto his heels. The kids said, "You can rock and roll with Mr. Crowell."

Cassie liked Mr. Crowell because he didn't smirk when she asked questions.

When it was animal-care time, Joe stood up and sighed and looked at Cassie.

"You don't mind cleaning animal cages, do you? I guess you really like that animal stuff." He walked slowly to the hamster cages.

The science room had more books on animals than even the regular school library. While Joe was cleaning the hamster cages, Cassie took several books about dogs to her seat.

When she started looking through the dog books, she realized that she couldn't describe the white dog very well. She had only seen him sitting down for less than a minute. She remembered his thick white fur, his long thin front legs, and his pointed ears with the shining halo. But she didn't really know how big he was or what he looked like when he stood up. Slowly she turned the pages.

Joe looked over her shoulder. "Oh, doggie books. Wanna find your doggie's picture?"

"I don't have a dog." She sighed. "I wish I did. I'm just looking."

"*I* have a dog. I named him Skunk because he's black and has a white stripe down his front."

"You mean skunk, like the animal?"

"Yeah."

Cassie smiled. "What kind of a dog is he?"

"Very special. Half of him is mongrel, and the other half is mutt." He laughed, and the girls near Cassie stirred and looked around. "Why don't you have a dog if you want one?"

"They cost too much," she said in a low voice.

"Whaddaya mean they cost too much!" exclaimed Joe. "You can get a dog practically for free at the pound if you pay for his shots and stuff. That's where we got Skunk."

"I mean to take care of. Dog food."

"Naaah," said Joe. "Skunk hardly ever has to eat dog food. We give him leftovers from the table." He looked at Cassie and grinned. "Course there's prob'ly no leftovers at your house." He added quickly, "Just kidding."

Cassie's face burned. She bent over her book. The pictures and the letters wiggled like worms, but she pretended to read while her mind shouted, "I hate him! I hate him!"

Only faintly she heard Mr. Crowell begin talking about how you couldn't save endangered animals unless you saved the lands and waters that the animals lived on. She didn't look in Joe's direction anymore. When class was over, she went up to Mr. Crowell's desk and signed out the dog books.

After school she always stopped at Daisy's Ice Cream Parlor for a single-scoop cone of chocolate fudge crunchie ice cream. As she neared the ice cream parlor, she wondered if the white dog liked chocolate fudge crunchie. Maybe she would save him the tip of her cone with ice cream in it. It would be his dessert after the ground beef.

She started to smile but suddenly shivered.

What if he was really *hungry?* What if he was lost, and the peanut butter and cookie sandwich she had left for him yesterday was the only food he had eaten all day? It was a good thing she had saved some ground beef for him last night.

C H A P T E R
4

Cassie couldn't imagine anything worse than being hungry and not having enough to eat.

Outside the ice cream parlor she hesitated, staring at the kids inside crowding up to the shining counter with its big tubs of many flavored ice creams.

A dog that beautiful couldn't be a stray. Surely someone somewhere was feeding him what he ought to have. Cassie licked her lips and put her hand on the door.

But what if he *was* lost? What if he really *was* hungry? A big dog like that needed more than just a little ground beef and part of an ice cream cone. She drew back, frowning. Several students brushed by her on their way into the parlor.

"Outta the way, Porky," said one. Cassie barely heard him. What was she going to do about feeding the white dog?

As she turned away she caught sight of a truck driving slowly along by the curb. On the side panel she read "County Animal Control." Her heart lurched. That meant the dog catcher, the same truck her mother had seen.

The white dog was the only dog she had seen

running loose in their neighborhood. He must be the dog they were looking for. She would have to make friends with him quickly and find a place to hide him. He couldn't end up in the pound!

She turned and hurried down the street to the corner grocery store. Its name was the Castleton Market, but some of the letters on the front window were missing so that it read CA TLETON ARKET. Cassie stepped inside and let her eyes adjust.

"Can I help you?" asked a thin man wearing glasses, a droopy moustache, and an apron. He had

been sweeping the floor, and he rested his hands on the long handle of the broom.

Cassie's voice always started out in a squeak when she had to talk to people she didn't know. She cleared her throat. "Where's the canned dog food?"

"Second aisle over, on the end." The clerk pointed.

Cassie walked down the aisles to the pet food and studied the different labels. Dog food was more expensive than she had thought it would be. She chose a can and quickly counted out her ice-cream money at the cash register. She put the can in her backpack and hurried home. The dog catcher truck was nowhere in sight.

On her way home, Cassie laid her plans. There was a better chance of the white dog's coming back, she thought, if everything was the same as when he first appeared. He probably had been attracted by the smell of food.

She was thinking so hard about the white dog and the dog catcher that just three doors from home she almost ran into Miss Kimura's gardener on the sidewalk. He was running his leaf-blower machine among the drifts of leaves fallen from the two big sycamore trees in her front yard.

"Watch where ya goin'!" shouted the gardener, waving the nozzle of the blower at her. "I'll blow ya away, I will, if ya run me down."

"I'm sorry," squeaked Cassie, stepping quickly out of the way onto the driveway.

"She's all right where she is," called a woman's voice.

Cassie looked up to where the slender figure of Miss Kimura stood leaning against the porch rail, watching. Cassie's mouth went dry. She stepped back on the sidewalk uncertainly.

Cassie sometimes saw Miss Kimura leaving her house early in the morning, Cassie guessed to go to work. She was Japanese, and Cassie thought she was pretty. She was younger than Cassie's mother, with long dark hair and smart-looking clothes. She drove a new gold-colored Lexus, and Cassie's mother sometimes wondered out loud what work a girl that young could do that paid so well.

Miss Kimura called out to Cassie, "Don't pay any attention to him. He won't hurt you."

Cassie wasn't sure about that, but she kept walking on the sidewalk toward home.

As she came near the gardener, he muttered, "Crazy lady. Don't like the blowin'. I'm gonna quit."

The last thing Cassie wanted the gardener to do was to quit working for Miss Kimura because of anything Cassie had done. She didn't want Miss Kimura mad at her; she lived only three doors away. The white dog might be walking through Miss Kimura's yard too. She turned to the gardener and squeaked, "Please don't quit. She needs you." She walked on, amazed at her courage in speaking up.

Cassie unlocked the front door and locked it again behind her. The house felt empty. How nice it would be to open the door and be welcomed by a dog!

She made herself a triple-decker sandwich and set it beside her books and papers on her work table.

Steadily she worked her way through the sandwich along with her homework. At a quarter to six, she closed her books.

In the kitchen, she opened the can of dog food. She found a metal mixing bowl in the cupboard and put half of the dog food into it, topped it off with the fresh ground beef she had saved, and hid the dog-food can on the bottom shelf at the back of the refrigerator where her mother wouldn't see it. Outside, she put the dish carefully under the tree.

She hurried to get the peanut butter, the caramel sauce, and what was left of the chocolate chips along with the box of sugar cookies. With the food arranged beside her as before, she sat down on the top step.

Cassie went through the motions of her scientific experiment of the day before, fixing the cookie sandwich, but her senses were tuned to the spot beneath the liquidambar tree where she had put the dog food. She sat holding the sandwich, watching the dish.

The sun dipped toward the hilltop and shone through the leaves of the liquidambar. Still the white dog didn't appear. Cassie felt a lump in her throat.

"Now," she whispered. "I brought you some food. Wherever you are, please come back. I want to be your friend. I won't let them take you to the pound."

She closed her eyes and kept thinking of how much she wanted the white dog to come back. When she opened her eyes, nothing had changed. There was no sign of the white dog. She didn't realize until then how much she had counted on his coming back.

What had made her think he would return? Why should a stray dog, passing through her yard, come back to a place where all he got was a little teeny peanut butter sandwich made of sugar cookies?

Her hands lay in her lap and she stared, unseeing, at the liquidambars. They blurred before her eyes. Through the blur, she saw what looked like white smoke appear in the shadows. She blinked.

It wasn't smoke. It was the white dog.

He advanced slowly, one step at a time, toward the dish with the dog food. Cassie hardly dared to breathe. The dog was watching something beyond her, but she didn't want to look away. Now she could see that his eyes were almond shaped and tilted. He looked like the sled dogs in the Iditarod races. He wasn't just handsome, he was exotic, mysterious.

"I'm glad you came back," she said softly.

He cocked his head a little to one side, and his tail swung slightly. He took one more step, and the last of the sun touched the top of his head. Again he wore a halo.

"You are beautiful," whispered Cassie. "You are the most beautiful dog in the world."

His tail swung partway, and his head went down to the dog food. He sniffed at it, put one huge paw on the side of the dish, and tipped it over. Then he nosed the food around in the dirt before he ate it. In one gulp, the ground beef was eaten; in two more gulps the canned food was gone.

Cassie stared. "You really *were* hungry!" she exclaimed. "I wish I'd known." She started to get up, but the white dog instantly drew back, one forepaw in the air.

Cassie sat down quickly. "I'll stay here. Don't worry. I won't hurt you. I want to be your friend."

This time his tail swung hard back and forth. He partly closed his slanted eyes, and his lips wrinkled up in a grin, the left side higher than the right so his grin was lopsided, almost impish. Cassie saw his white teeth for an instant and was startled to see how big they were. His long pink tongue almost wrapped itself around his muzzle as he licked his chops.

"I'll feed you again tomorrow," she said. "Please come back again, and I'll feed you more."

He must have been mistreated, she thought, to be so afraid of people. Another thought occurred to her. What if he wasn't just lost? What if whoever owned him was mean to him? What if he had been beaten and had run away? She shivered. Suddenly becoming this dog's friend was more important than anything else.

"Not all people are bad," she told him. "You can trust me. You'll see." She smiled.

The dog swung his tail again, turned, and melted into the shadows. He was gone.

CHAPTER
5

Cassie wanted to sing out loud and dance for joy. The dog would be her friend. It was the beginning of friendship.

She hastily ate the cookie in her hand, went into the house, and put away her supplies. With the *Complete Dog Book* propped upon her pillow, she stretched out on her bed. Slowly she turned the pages.

The *Complete Dog Book* had pictures of every breed of dog recognized by kennel clubs around the world, including some dogs that Cassie had never heard of. But there wasn't a single breed that was exactly like the white dog. The two that resembled him the most were the Alaskan malamute and the Siberian husky. Cassie had always lumped them together as Eskimo dogs, the ones that ran in the Iditarod races.

The Alaskan malamute was the biggest, about the right size, and his face looked the most like the white dog's, but that's where the resemblance stopped. The white dog was streamlined, with legs unusually long and thin. The malamute was really stocky.

The Siberian husky in the picture was pure white

ALASKAN MALAMUTE

SIBERIAN HUSKY

like her dog. Cassie read on. "The Siberian husky is naturally friendly and gentle in temperament. They are intelligent, faithful, reliable, and known for their speed and endurance." She hoped her dog was a Siberian husky, but then she read the description. Her dog was much too tall and thin.

None of the pictures looked like her white dog.

The white dog was terribly thin. He must have been on the road a long time, hiding out and scrounging for food. Cassie frowned. What would he look like after he'd been fed for a while? She went through the book a second time. His picture was not there. She decided to tell Mr. Crowell about the stray dog and ask for his help.

The next day she could hardly wait to get to school and talk to Mr. Crowell. He knew so much about animals that surely he would know what kind of a dog it was.

She watched for the animal control truck but didn't see it anywhere. She breathed a sigh of relief.

In the science room before class, the boys had gathered around Brad Keeler. Cassie could see his blond head above all the others. Brad was bragging about going hunting next weekend. He had his tag for deer, whatever that meant, though Cassie could tell it didn't mean anything good for a deer.

When the bell rang for class to begin and everyone took their places, Cassie saw that Brad was wearing camouflage pants and heavy boots that laced. He swaggered to his desk. She saw Mr. Crowell frowning, but he didn't say anything.

During science class, she checked out two more dog books. When the bell rang at the end of class and the students stampeded out of the room, Cassandra lingered by Mr. Crowell's desk. He looked up.

"A couple of days ago, a big white dog came into our yard," she began. Her voice never squeaked when she was talking with Mr. Crowell. "He was really beautiful. I've never seen any dog like him. I wondered what kind he is."

"Tell me about him."

She said carefully, "Well, he looks like an Eskimo dog, you know, the dogs in the Alaskan sled races, but I think he's taller. His legs are real long and thin. His fur is very thick, especially around his neck, and he's pure white. His fur's so white it shines like silver." Mr. Crowell nodded as she spoke and slowly rocked up and down. "He has a longish muzzle and pointed ears," she felt her voice take on a feeling of awe, "and his eyes are slanted."

Mr. Crowell smiled. "He certainly does sound like some kind of sled dog—Alaskan malamute or Siberian husky. You've looked in the American Kennel Club book?"

She nodded. "I can't find any dog exactly like him. He looks almost like a malamute, but he's too tall and thin. He's too big to be any of the other Eskimo dogs."

Mr. Crowell nodded thoughtfully. "Could he be a cross between a malamute and another breed?"

"I suppose it's possible, but I don't think so,"

Cassandra said quickly. "He doesn't look like a mongrel."

Mr. Crowell studied her face. "You can't tell if a dog is purebred just by looking at him."

"But he's so aristocratic." She cleared her throat. "I've never seen . . ." Her voice trailed off.

"Are you sure the AKC book you used is the latest edition? They've just recognized some exotic new breeds."

Cassie nodded. "I even went through a book that had breeds recognized by other countries. I couldn't find anything that looked exactly like him."

Mr. Crowell considered this. "Have you looked in the lost and found column of the newspaper?"

Cassie felt her stomach lurch. "No, I hadn't thought of that. Anyway, we don't subscribe to the newspaper. Mom says she wouldn't have time to read it." She felt sick. It had never occurred to her that whoever owned him would advertise. She had thought only of how scared she thought he was.

"There might be a reward."

"Oh." She felt even worse. She wanted the dog, not a reward. But what if his owners had advertised for him, and someone who wasn't his owner but wanted the reward saw the dog going by? She spoke quickly. "All I know is he's awfully hungry, so I've started feeding him."

"He's come to your house more than once?"

Cassie hesitated. "I was on the back porch having a snack, and he smelled the food and came into the yard, so I fed him. Yesterday I bought a can of dog food, and he came back and I gave him half of it. I'll give him the other half this afternoon."

Mr. Crowell gazed out the window. "But he must be missed. I'll look in the papers when I get home this evening. A dog as beautiful as you say he is must belong to someone."

"But then why is he so scared?" protested Cassie. "I think he's run away. You should see how scared he is. I can't get anywhere near him yet. It will be a long time before I can pet him. Someone hasn't treated him right." She found herself trembling. "I'll treat him right." She took a deep breath and rushed on. "I want to feed him every day because I want him to adopt me."

Mr. Crowell looked at her again. "Yes, well, until you find the owner, you certainly ought to feed him. In the meantime, I'll watch the lost and found column."

"Oh. Thanks." She hoped there wouldn't be an ad. She didn't want the owners to get him back. If they had been good to him, he wouldn't be so scared. They didn't deserve such a beautiful animal. How could people be so mean to animals? She suddenly thought of Brad Keeler and his camouflage suit.

She drew a deep breath and said, "Mr. Crowell, can't you do something about Brad Keeler and his always bragging about hunting? He likes *killing* animals."

Mr. Crowell pursed his lips for a minute. "He's

doing what is legal as far as hunting is concerned, so no one can stop him. And it's not against the law to brag."

"But *why* does he go hunting?"

Mr. Crowell frowned. "He told me it's a family sport."

"A family sport!" exclaimed Cassie.

"That's what he says. His whole family, he and his parents and his brother, all go hunting on weekends. They camp out in the forest, cook their own meals, and have a great time together."

For the first time, Cassie felt a pang. Her family had never done anything together like that. She remembered the trip to the circus she had taken with her father while her mother had stayed home. If only Brad could find something to do with his family besides hunting. At least she could understand Brad having fun going out in the woods with his family. She sighed. Another thought crossed her mind.

"How can it be a real sport if the animals don't have guns and can't shoot back?"

A brief smile flickered over Mr. Crowell's face. "Perhaps he'd like to tell you his side of hunting."

"I don't want to hear it. I think he's just trying to be macho, like a lot of the guys."

"We'll see."

Cassandra bypassed Daisy's Ice Cream Parlor and started home very slowly, thinking in despair about the lost and found column and the animal control truck. When she was depressed, chocolate usually cheered her up. She wondered how much chocolate she would have to eat before her stomach stopped hurting.

As soon as she got home, she went through her hiding places until she found part of a box of Hershey almond bars. She took three of them and settled herself with her homework, munching as she worked. Slowly the pain in her stomach began to ease.

As soon as her watch told her it was time for the white dog's supper, she fixed the last half of the canned dog food and carried the dish out to the liquidambar tree. She sat quietly on the bottom step and waited.

She didn't have to wait long. The white dog appeared out of nowhere, approached the dish cautiously, sniffed its contents, and again pushed it over with his paw to spill out the food.

"You silly dog," said Cassie, watching him push the canned food around on the ground before eating it. "Maybe you don't like eating out of a dish." She wondered if she should just dump the food on the ground next time. Then she realized she would have to buy another can of dog food at the Catleton Arket.

When the dog finished his meal, he licked his chops with his long tongue and then crouched on his forepaws facing Cassie. He stuck his rump up in the air and swung his tail back and forth. It was almost as though he were taking a bow. Suddenly he grinned his lopsided grin.

"You're thanking me!" she exclaimed. "You're very

welcome! I'll feed you tomorrow, same time, same place."

He bounced up and down several times, making funny little whining and squeaking noises, then turned and melted into the bushes as silently as he had appeared.

"Whew!" said Cassandra happily. She went inside to read the dog books she had brought home.

One of the books listed advantages and disadvantages of each of the breeds and even told how much food they needed. She was shocked when she read how much a big dog would eat. For a malamute or a husky, a half a can of food was nothing, *nothing*. Her white dog would have to have at least two cans of dog food every day and a couple of pounds of dry kibble. How could she possibly feed him that much?

Cassie received a variable allowance from her mother. It was supposed to be a fixed amount, but how much she actually got depended on the tips her mother collected. Her mother kept part of the tip money to use for "running the household," but if Cassie needed something extra, her mother was usually good for a soft touch. Cassie had liked it that way because she figured she collected more. She packed her own lunch every day and always bought something extra at the snack lines.

But now the hard facts were staring her in the face. Even if Cassie didn't buy any more snacks, which was unthinkable, and gave up buying pencils and paper and school stuff, which she had to have, there wasn't enough money. Even if she didn't buy anything extra at all and saved every penny of her allowance, she still wouldn't have enough money to buy food for her white dog. Cassie took a deep breath and shuddered. She realized she needed more money than she'd ever had before, and she didn't dare ask her mother.

She would have to find a job.

CHAPTER
6

During study hall the next day, Cassie made a list of things the job must do and must not do. Being scientific did have some advantages, she thought. It helped her get organized. She looked at her list with satisfaction. These were all the things the job must do:

1. Must pay enough to buy all the dog food.
2. Must pay daily or weekly.
3. Must be outside of school hours.
4. Must be within walking distance.
5. Must pay in cash. I hope.

The second part had only one item:

1. Must not work for anyone who will tell M.

"M" was her mother. When Cassie applied for work, she would say she needed the job to buy food for a dog that she was getting. Her working to feed a dog might be appealing to a possible employer. That meant she couldn't work for anyone who might tell her mother. Her mother would call the dog pound.

Cassie wasn't sure how to start looking for a job. She knew the paper wouldn't carry ads for work for a thirteen-year-old, so there was no point in borrowing a paper from someone or looking through it. She needed to talk to a grown-up. Mr. Crowell might be willing to help.

She stood by his desk after science class, and he smiled.

"So how's your white dog? Did he come back?"

"Oh, yes. You should have seen him gulp down his supper. I read in one of the dog books a big dog like that needs an awful lot of food, but I can't ask Mom for money. Even if I don't get to keep him, I need some kind of job to pay for his food right now."

Mr. Crowell nodded. "I can see you have a problem." He fidgeted with a notebook on his desk. "Offhand, I can't think of anyone needing work that you could do."

Cassie felt a pang. She had secretly hoped Mr. Crowell would hire her himself. "Don't you have any animals at home that need taking care of sometimes?"

He shook his head. "I don't keep any animals at home. All my animals are here, in the science room."

"Oh." She tried not to show her disappointment.

"Maybe one of the other teachers will have something for you to do. I'll ask around."

"Oh, please do, Mr. Crowell."

She still had enough money to buy some kind of dog food. She went from school directly to the Catleton Arket.

"More dog food?" asked the clerk, nodding. "Cheaper than canned food? Sure, we got dog kibble."

He pointed to some large sacks stacked along the wall behind the cashier's stand.

Cassie studied the price tags on the sacks of kibble. It was cheaper by the pound, but she didn't have enough for a whole sack. She cleared her throat. "I guess I'll just have another can."

"What kind of dog you got?"

Cassie shrugged. "Just a big dog. But he eats a lot."

"Yup, they do."

Desperation gripped Cassie. "Say, is there any kind of work I could do here to earn money for the dog food? For a sack of kibble? I'm good at sorting and arranging stuff in order. I get straight As in my science class."

The clerk looked at her as though for the first time. "I dunno. You'd have to ask Mr. Ulmer; he's the owner. He's out back talking to a delivery man. He'll be here in a minute."

Cassie found her breath getting short and her heart pounding. Her palms were sweaty. She was suddenly aware she had on her oldest worn jeans and one of her un-favorite shirts. She certainly wasn't dressed for applying for a job. She hadn't even combed her hair. She wasn't ready.

The clerk spoke up cheerfully. "Here he comes now."

Cassie took one look at the man entering the back door and fled. She was halfway home before she realized she hadn't even bought the can of dog food.

Cassie looked at herself in the mirror over her dresser and trembled. She absolutely had to go back to the store to buy the dog food. No other market was in walking distance.

But talk to Mr. Ulmer about a job? Who would want to hire a chubby girl with stringy brown hair and perspiration dripping on her face?

Cassie stared at herself in the mirror and tilted up her chin. She went into the bathroom and turned on the shower in the tub. Twenty minutes later, she towel dried her hair as she went over in her mind just what she would say to Mr. Ulmer if she did ask him for a job. From her closet, she chose her newest pair of jeans and her best blue tee shirt with a poodle on it. At least it would show she was interested in dogs.

If she could buy just one big sack of kibble to start with. . . . She marched out of the house and down the street, breathing hard with determination.

She hadn't counted on meeting Shannon and Joanna on her way to the store. They whispered to each other, and Cassie started to glare at them. But what if later she needed their help with the white dog? She smiled as cheerfully as she could and stepped out of their way. The smirks vanished, and she thought their faces seemed almost friendly. She thought about that as she pushed open the door to the Catleton Arket.

"What happened to you?" asked the clerk. "I told Mr. Ulmer you was lookin' fer a job." He turned and called out, "Here's that girl wanted to see you."

Cassie swallowed hard. Mr. Ulmer had a beer belly that pushed his plaid shirt out over his belt, a pudgy, wrinkled face with pale blue eyes that blinked quite often, and thinning gray hair brushed carefully over the bald part of his head.

"What do you want?" he asked in a mild voice.

Cassie breathed more easily and cleared her throat. Her voice wobbled, but it didn't squeak. "I want a job. I'm going to get a dog, but I have to earn the money to feed him. Please can I work for you?" She knew that wasn't businesslike. "I mean, I'm a straight-A student in science, and I'm good at organizing and sorting and putting things away and stuff. I'm a good worker." That was true, provided she was interested in the work.

Mr. Ulmer looked her up and down. "How old are you?"

She wanted to say "Sixteen," but Cassie knew if she said sixteen and later they found out she was in eighth grade, they might think she'd flunked a grade or two. "Thirteen. I'm in eighth grade." Too young to work at a regular job, she knew.

Mr. Ulmer smiled gently. "I don't have any work in the store for you, but Mrs. Ulmer was looking for someone to weed our front lawn. Her arthritis bothers her, and she can't do the gardening like she used to."

"I *love* to garden," said Cassie. "When can I start?"

Mr. Ulmer made a noise like a chuckle. "I don't know your name, or where you live, or how much you charge."

"Oh." Cassie felt her face turn pink. "I'm Cassandra Beasley, and I live three blocks down on

Larkspur Lane. I don't know how much to charge."
Now that was dumb, she thought.

Mr. Ulmer laughed out loud. It wasn't the kind of
laugh that comes with making fun of someone. It
was the sort of laugh between friends. "We live in
the first house around the corner. Mrs. Ulmer's home
right now. Why don't you go talk to her?"

"Oh." Cassie gulped. "Yes, I will. Right away." She
started off before she remembered her manners.
"Thank you very much."

She hurried out the door and around the corner.
The Ulmers lived in a very small, tan stucco house
surrounded by a patchy lawn that needed both water
and weeding. Some drooping rose bushes lined the
cement walk leading to the front door. Cassie's heart
pounded, but she walked to the porch, took two
steps up, and bravely rang the doorbell.

The door opened, and Mrs. Ulmer stood there,
one skinny hand patting at her frizzy gray hair. "Who
are you and what do you want?"

Cassie cleared her throat and said in a rush, "I'm
Cassie Beasley from three blocks down on Larkspur
Lane and Mr. Ulmer said you wanted somebody to do
some gardening for you and I need the job because
I'm getting a dog and I have to earn the money to pay
for the dog food." Cassie listened to herself with astonishment. She had never before said so many
words at once even to her mother, much less to a
total stranger.

Mrs. Ulmer opened her mouth and then closed it

again. She smiled. "Are you a good worker? Do you like gardening?"

Cassie took a deep breath. "I'm a *very* good worker. I love gardening, and I'll work hard because my dog eats a lot."

"You said you were getting a dog. You already have him?"

Cassie thought fast. "I get to keep him if I can pay for his food. He eats more than I thought he would."

Mrs. Ulmer nodded. "That's usually what happens. I'll try you out and see if you're the kind of gardener I need. I'll pay you four dollars an hour." She walked across the porch and motioned to the one-car garage at the side of the house. "There are gardening tools in there. I suppose you'd like to start as soon as possible."

"Oh yes!" Cassie burst out.

Mrs. Ulmer smiled. "How about tomorrow after school?"

"You bet. I mean, as soon as I change into some gardening clothes. I'll be here about four o'clock if that's okay."

Mrs. Ulmer nodded again. "First come in the house and write down your name and address and phone number so I can get in touch with you if I need to."

She held the door open, and Cassie stepped inside.

CHAPTER
7

Cassie looked around her. Too much furniture crowded the little house. There were straight-backed chairs and easy chairs and rocking chairs. There were empty bookcases and end tables and coffee tables. There were even two hall tables side by side that didn't match.

Mrs. Ulmer pulled a piece of paper from a drawer in one of the hall tables and offered a pen to Cassie. "And put down any references you might have."

"References?" asked Cassie.

"Yes. You know, someone you've worked for before. Someone who knows you and can tell me about your character."

Cassie gulped. "This is my first job." She brightened. "My science teacher, Mr. Crowell, knows my character. He'll recommend me, I'm sure. I can ask him for his phone number."

"That's a good idea," said Mrs. Ulmer. She looked at the paper when Cassie had finished. "You don't live far away."

"No, I don't. It will be easy for me to come here."

Mrs. Ulmer smiled. "Well, if you do a good job,

you'll be just the person I've been looking for. Tomorrow I'll show you what I want done."

"Great!" said Cassie with enthusiasm. "I'll see you tomorrow."

Cassie returned to the Catleton Arket and bought a can of dog food. Mr. Ulmer was at the cash register.

"So. How did your interview go?"

"I've got the job. I start tomorrow. And thank you *very* much for telling me about it."

Mr. Ulmer nodded, smiling gently. "I hope it works out. And I hope your dog gets enough to eat."

"He will! I'll see to that!" She put the dog food in her backpack. She would have skipped all the way home if she could, but she was content to hurry in a sort of running walk.

In the last block before home, the County Animal Control truck drove by slowly. When it stopped at the stop sign, Cassie was too curious to walk past. With her heart pounding, she went over to the truck and looked in the window. The driver was an attractive woman with short dark hair cut almost like a boy's. She didn't look anything like Cassie's idea of a dog catcher, except that she wore a blue uniform.

Cassie said, "Are you looking for anything special?"

The woman frowned at Cassie. "We've had several reports of a big white dog running around loose in this neighborhood. I don't suppose you've seen him." It was more a statement than a question.

Cassie tried to look nonchalant. "Everybody around here tries to keep their dogs on a leash."

The control officer nodded. "I thought so. I've been on patrol for three days, and I haven't seen any without a leash."

"Isn't it hard being a dog catcher?" Cassie blurted. She hadn't meant to say that. She held her breath, waiting for the driver to get mad.

The woman looked at Cassie and smiled. "I've saved a lot of animals in my job. I've rescued dogs from the irrigation canal and cats from trees, and I've saved horses who were being starved by stupid owners. It's not just catching dogs. I don't really like the name dog catcher."

"Oh," said Cassie. "Maybe we should call you Animal Rescue instead of Animal Control."

The officer laughed. "I'll remember that. Thanks." As the truck drove off, Cassie turned and walked to her house, her heart thumping with anxiety. So someone had reported her white dog, but the dog catcher hadn't found him. She might have to hide the white dog in her house.

She unlocked the front door and realized with amazement that she had talked to three total strangers, told two of them about her dog, and asked for a job and got it. Her first job, after the very first interview! That beautiful white dog would be able to eat all he wanted. He would be her very own dog— if no one advertised for him.

She began to wonder how long she could keep her mother from finding out about the dog. Her mother worked the day shift at the Red Baron Burger, so on work days the dog would eat before her mother got home. But what would Cassie do on her mother's two days off each week?

She longed to be able to tell her mother about her job at the Ulmers'. How happy her mother would be to know Cassie was showing responsibility by getting a job. But then her mother would think she spent the money on more junk food and candy, and she would get mad. Cassie sighed.

From her closet shelf, she took a package of Oreo cookies and put them beside her school books. She liked to separate the two halves, lick off the filling, and eat the cookies, one at a time. She plodded through her homework, munching as she worked.

When it was five-thirty, she said happily out loud, "Almost time to feed . . ." She stopped. Her dog didn't have a name, and he needed one. Something different, a name no other dog ever had. He would learn to come when she called him.

Cassie went into the kitchen and opened the new can of dog food. She emptied all of it into the dog dish. She washed the can, squashed it flat, and put it where her mother couldn't see it underneath other squashed cans at the bottom of the box marked "cans only."

All the while, her mind was skipping ahead, making plans for her dog. Tomorrow at school, she would look up a map of Alaska. There ought to be a name that sounded unusual.

She carried the dog dish outside to the liquid-ambar tree and retreated to the bottom step.

She sat down and fixed her eyes on the dish by the tree. He had come twice now. She was sure he would come again.

Something moved behind the shrubs. It was the white dog, watching her with his head lowered and one forepaw raised. Cassie's heart skidded to a stop. He came around the corner of the bushes, ears partway back, head tilted to one side, tail swinging back and forth. His eyes almost closed as he wrinkled up his lips in his lopsided grin. He advanced cautiously to the dish, tipped it over, and pushed the food around on the ground before gulping it down. Cassie sat quietly, longing to pet the dog, to put her arms around him and hold him close.

When he finished eating and had licked his muzzle clean, he cocked his head sideways at Cassie and swung his tail harder. He came toward her then, slowly, one step at a time, and when he reached her, he began sniffing her carefully and thoroughly. Cassie sat perfectly still. He drew in short breaths and moved his nose up and down her jeans, each sock in turn, and then her shoes. He finished by checking out her cotton shirt, paying special attention to the pockets. Cassie nearly collapsed with delight. She took a deep breath, slowly reached out, and stroked him with both hands. His fur was thick and coarse and almost wirey, and it shone like silver. "How beautiful you are," she whispered.

He walked back and forth in front of her, pressing against her each time he passed. She tried to memorize exactly the way he looked. He was taller than

she had thought. She admired his long slender
muzzle, the huge ruff of fur around his neck, his thin,
aristocratic legs, and the way his big brush of a tail
swung back and forth. At last he turned and trotted
off, melting into the shadows.

Cassie felt like she was floating on a cloud. Three
times in a row her dog had come to her, and tonight
he had let her pet him. The most beautiful dog in the
world wanted to be her friend. She retrieved the dish
and sat for a long time, staring at the place where the
white dog had been.

Her mind raced with plans. She would fix a shelter for him nearby so he'd have a place to sleep. He would need a collar, so everyone would know he wasn't a stray. Somehow he would have to get his shots at the vet's. And a dog license. And a little tag in the shape of a heart with his name on it. An unusual name, from Alaska. Tomorrow, at school, she would choose his name.

She stood up and took the empty dish into the house to wash and put away. She carried the cookies into the living room and settled herself on the couch in front of the TV.

I have a beautiful dog, she kept saying to herself. The most beautiful white dog in the world belongs to me.

She forgot to reach for the cookies. She watched the news as if in a trance. Even the flood scenes from the other county were boring—her own life was more exciting. She stared at her favorite show that followed, and afterward couldn't remember a thing that happened.

The front door opened and her mother said, "Hi, I'm home," in her tired voice.

"Oh hi, Mom," Cassie said, trying to keep her voice steady. She got up and started toward the kitchen. "Have you had supper?"

Her mother nodded. "Yeah. You don't have to fix anything for me. I ate at work so I could talk to a couple of the other girls. Some people sure have a lot of problems. I don't know why they always like to unload them on me."

Cassie didn't know either. Her mother not only didn't *understand* Cassie's problems, but her mother *was* her problem.

Cassie wondered what to fix for her own supper. There were several packages of ground beef in the refrigerator, but she wanted to save as much as she could for her dog. Grilled cheese sandwiches would be okay.

After supper she went back to her room and leafed through the AKC book again. Her dog certainly wasn't in the book. Tomorrow she would take out some books on Alaska.

CHAPTER
8

In the morning, Cassie packed her lunch, saving what she thought the dog would like. When study hall came around, she headed for the library and the atlas. She turned to the map of Alaska.

A lot of the names were in plain English—Sterling, Crooked Creek, Swift Fork, Farewell, Fairbanks. But then there were Chatanika, Nenana, Anvik, and a mountain named Kuskowim. Just in case, she checked out two books on Alaska. She wanted to know more about where her dog came from.

After science class, Mr. Crowell beckoned Cassie to his desk.

"How's your white dog?" he asked.

Cassie was excited over her progress. "Yesterday he let me pet him! He came at the same time, and I gave him another can of dog food. I've got a job gardening for Mrs. Ulmer after school, and I'll be able to buy all the food he needs." She smiled happily. Then she remembered. "Mrs. Ulmer asked me for references, and I wondered if you'd let me give her your name and phone number."

Mr. Crowell smiled. "I'd be happy to." He wrote on a piece of paper and handed it to Cassie. "She can call me any evening." Cassie tucked the note in the pocket of her jeans. Mr. Crowell rocked forward on his toes and then back and said, "I've been reading the classifieds."

Cassie's stomach did a nosedive.

He went on. "There's been nothing in the lost and found," he said. Cassie felt a smile spread over her face. "Of course the dog might be from a completely different area."

"That means he could be lost."

"Quite possibly."

"So no one knows he's around here." She felt lighthearted. "Well, I'll take good care of him till his owners come to get him."

Mr. Crowell picked up two books on his desk and handed them to Cassie. "I stopped by the public library last night," he said almost apologetically, "and it occurred to me there might be something more about sled dogs. I found these."

One was on the Alaskan malamute, the other was on the Alaskan people. Cassie, pleased, thanked him and went back to her desk. Now she had three books on Alaska and one on the Alaskan dog.

Joe Pinatelli peered over her shoulder. "Oh, now it's Eskimo dogs. You gonna get an Eskimo dog? Cool. How come you're so interested in Eskimos?"

She smiled. "Alaska is awfully interesting. Haven't you seen the Iditarod sled races on TV?"

"Yeah, sure! Those are some dogs. They say some of them are part wolf."

Cassie was startled. Well, maybe her dog did look

a little bit like a picture she had seen of a wolf, as well as she could remember.

"Hey, if you get a dog from Alaska, how you going to keep him cool in the summer?"

"I don't know. I hadn't thought about that," Cassie said truthfully. "Have you got any ideas?" Immediately she braced herself for some rude remark from Joe. When would she learn to keep her mouth shut?

Joe chewed on his lower lip. "Well, you could rig up a sort of sprinkler for him with a hose. You know, like the little kids do in the summer when it's real hot. He could play in the sprinklers."

She pictured her white dog playing in the sprinklers. She almost giggled. "That's a great idea."

"Can't you just see that Eskimo dog playing in the sprinklers?" said Joe, and they burst into laughter.

The students near them turned to look.

"Quiet, please, back there," said Mr. Crowell.

Both of them bent over their books. Cassie busied herself for a minute and then sneaked a glance at Joe. He was still smiling as he turned a page.

Joe's sprinkler idea was a good one. It's true that the dog would be awfully hot in the summer in California with that thick white fur. Of course she would still have him by summer.

Her imagination spun a whole story. Maybe her dog really was from Alaska and he had been in the Iditarod race. And he had been brought to California to be in the movies because he was so beautiful. Last year Cassie had read about some compounds in a nearby county where animals were trained for the movies. Maybe her dog's owners were taking him to one of those compounds, and he jumped out of their car when they weren't looking. His owners didn't know he had jumped out and had no idea where they had lost him.

Maybe Joe was right and her dog was part wolf. He was scared being in a big city, and somehow he had found his way to Cassie's place because it was on the edge of town, almost in the country. That's why he was shy and took his time making friends with her. But now they really were friends.

She smiled, thinking of his letting her pet him, how he had leaned against her as a kind of thank you before he left. Imagine that. Maybe she was friends with a part wolf.

Toward the end of science class Cassie had a chance to look at the books. She skimmed a couple of paragraphs in the first one. Alaska was really an interesting place. It had gained statehood in 1959, but most of it still wasn't settled. There were many remote villages too small to be on any map. One village, called Toklata, caught her eye. That would be a cool name for an Alaskan dog. Her dog. She could call him Tokie for short.

Next she flipped open *The Alaskan Malamute* by somebody Gordon. In all the pictures, the malamutes had tails that curled up over their backs. Her dog couldn't be a malamute. His tail hung down straight when he wasn't swinging it.

Well, if the dog wasn't a malamute, he could still be a sled dog for racing. Cassie glanced down the page. There was a lot of debate about where the malamute came from. Was the malamute a direct descendant of the wolf? Was it a wolf crossed with some kind of Spitz? Or was it a descendant of a dog brought into Alaska by Asian immigrants? Cassie closed the book. If only she could find a picture that looked like her dog. She was glad it was Friday and she had the weekend to go through all the books.

As soon as school was out, Cassie hurried home. She unlocked her front door, dropped her backpack on the bed, and put the books on her desk. She quickly changed into the clothes she was going to use for gardening. Not her oldest grubby ones, but something comfortable that she'd still look sort of good in. She thought Mrs. Ulmer would like that.

In her backpack, she put some snacks to eat while she was working. She was going to fix herself a double-decker sandwich before she started out, but she glanced at her watch. It was later than she thought, and she didn't want to be late, especially on her first day at work. She hoisted the straps of the backpack over her shoulders and hurried down the street to the Ulmers'.

She rang the bell, and a minute later the door opened. Mrs. Ulmer patted her frizzy gray hair with one skinny hand and said, "Who are you and what do you want?"

Cassie's heart almost stopped. "I'm Cassandra Beasley, and yesterday you hired me to do some gardening for you. You asked me to start today."

Mrs. Ulmer's face had a vacant look. She gazed

past Cassie and then looked at her again. Her eyes seemed to suddenly focus. "Oh yes, I remember."

Cassie said, "You wanted me to bring a reference, so I did." She handed Mrs. Ulmer the piece of paper. "Here's Mr. Crowell's name and phone number. You can call him any evening."

Mrs. Ulmer smiled. "I'll do that." She motioned to the garage. "You'll find a trowel and anything else you might need in the garage just inside the door on the left. Here's what I want you to do." Cassie was to dig up all the weeds in the front lawn and put them in a big plastic garbage sack. Cassie looked around the yard. It must have been months, maybe years, since anyone had attacked the weeds. Good, thought Cassie. The more work, the more money to earn.

Cassie decided to attack the yard scientifically. In her mind, she marked off the yard in squares and determined to finish one square at a time, beginning with the one nearest the front porch. She set the plastic garbage sack beside her and jabbed the trowel into the hard dirt at the base of the first clump of dandelions. The ground was like cement. Again and again she jabbed. After seven tries, she pulled out some mangled dandelion leaves and roots with dirt on them. This was not going to be easy, she thought. In fact, it was terrible.

Within fifteen minutes, the palm of her right hand ached, and she hadn't even gotten across the top of the first square. If only she had gloves. She changed the trowel to her left hand and gritted her teeth. It was slower, but she kept on. Soon her left hand was as sore as her right hand. She suddenly realized that her back was one big sharp pain from twisting to attack the weeds. Her knees were numb from kneeling on the hard ground. Her hands were shaking, and they hurt. She hurt all over.

She laid down the trowel and slowly collapsed onto the ground. She studied her hands and saw funny white bumps on her palms. Blisters. Blisters!

She wasn't used to this kind of work. She didn't see how she could chop out another weed, much

less do the whole yard. How could she possibly go on? She could hardly move.

Her first job was impossible.

She couldn't earn the money to buy enough dog food for the beautiful white dog. She wouldn't be able to feed him, and he would start looking somewhere else for food. He would get hungrier and hungrier until he took chances in order to eat and some stranger caught him. And then he would go to the pound.

C H A P T E R
9

Two shoes appeared beside her as Cassie stared at the ground. She looked up into Mrs. Ulmer's frowning face.

"Hard work, isn't it?"

To Cassie's horror, she found herself sobbing. "I wanted this job so bad, and I can't do it." The sobs shook her whole body. "It's too hard."

"I didn't think you were a quitter."

Cassie, startled, looked up. She struggled to her feet while she considered what Mrs. Ulmer said. Well, maybe she did sort of quit trying when things were too hard. Like her classes at school except for science.

But this was different. Her white dog's life depended on it. She was *not* going to quit.

She had to think of a way to get the job done.

"No, I'm not quitting." She mopped her face on her sleeve and surveyed the yard. "If you'll let me water the lawn for half an hour, I won't charge you for it. Next time it'll be easier to pull the weeds out. And I'll get some gloves."

Mrs. Ulmer smiled. "That's better. Watering is part of gardening just the same, so I'll pay you for that.

I haven't bothered to water with all these weeds." She looked around and sighed. "This used to be so pretty."

"It will look pretty again, but it will take a while. Those roses will bloom better if they're dug up around their roots. I'll work hard," Cassie said earnestly.

"Keeping that dog is important to you," said Mrs. Ulmer.

Cassie snuffled and nodded.

"There are work gloves in the garage. I forgot to tell you. And there's a board with pads on it for kneeling. Mr. Ulmer fixed it for me before my arthritis got so bad. You might want to use it till the ground gets softer." She smiled. "I'm glad you're not going to quit."

"No ma'am," said Cassie. "You won't be sorry you hired me."

"Good. I've needed someone to help. Why don't you come in and sit down for a few minutes before you start watering? That weeding is very hard work."

"I found that out."

The two went into the house, and Cassie sat down carefully in one of the wooden rocking chairs. She was afraid that if she sat in an easy chair, she'd never be able to get out of it. She looked around at all the furniture. The house had a clean smell of furniture polish and wax.

"Would you like a glass of apple cider?"

"Oh yes, please." Suddenly she realized how thirsty she was. And hungry. She hadn't taken time out to eat her snack, she had been working so hard. Did she dare ask Mrs. Ulmer if she could bring in her backpack with the snack? No, that would be pushing her luck. How many gardeners get to sit in the owner's house and have something to drink?

Mrs. Ulmer handed her a tall glass of cider with ice cubes tinkling in it and said, "It's easy to get terribly attached to a dog. That's why I don't have one now. Parting with the last one was too painful."

"What happened to him?" asked Cassie, not really wanting to know.

"He was old, and he had trouble walking. He was nearly sixteen when he had to be put to sleep. Mr. Ulmer took him down to the vet's for me; I couldn't bear to say good-bye. I still miss him." There was a small silence. "I like cats, too. I've got three around here some place. Probably on my bed taking their afternoon nap."

"I love animals. I hope I can find some kind of work that has to do with animals."

"Dog walking?"

"No, I mean when I get out of college. If I can go to college. I want to study biology, but I don't want to take animals apart." A thought popped into her head. "I want to put them back together. But I don't mean as a veterinarian."

"What do you mean?"

"What I mean is, study them as a whole animal. Find out what's best for them. Like my dog. He's terribly scared of people, even me." She bit her tongue. She had said too much.

Mrs. Ulmer looked at her steadily. "Where did you get this dog? Is he really yours?"

Cassie sighed. "No ma'am. I guess you'd say he's a stray. He came into my yard a couple of days ago, and he's awfully thin. I've been feeding him. And he's so scared of people, it's been hard for me to get near him. He let me pet him yesterday for the first time. I want to be his friend."

"Have you looked in the lost and found?"

"No ma'am. We don't subscribe to a newspaper, but Mr. Crowell is watching it for me. So far there hasn't been anything. But I can tell the dog's been mistreated. I think he might have run away from where he lived."

"At least that's what you hope."

Cassie looked down at the rug. "I guess so." She stood up. "I'd better start watering the lawn."

There weren't any sprinklers, so she had to hold the nozzle of the hose and spray the water on the weeds, working her way from one imaginary square to another. She put extra water on the first three squares where she planned to start weeding next time.

"That ought to do it," she said at last with satisfaction and coiled up the hose by the garage.

Mrs. Ulmer stood by the front door. "It looks better in just one hour. Don't you think that's enough for today?"

Cassie nodded solemnly. She couldn't have bent over one more weed for a million dollars.

Mrs. Ulmer said, "Let me pay you for today." She

went in the house and returned with her purse. "I think until this yard gets whipped into shape, I'd like to have you come every day, if you can. Except Sunday."

"Sure, I'd like that a lot." So Mrs. Ulmer liked her work. She was a success!

"Suppose I pay you each time to start with. That will give you what you need for your dog. Then later we can make it once a week, if that's all right with you."

"That sounds great." She took the four one-dollar bills and held them in her hand with a strange feeling. Her first really earned money, not handed to her by her mother or her father. "Thank you very much." She stuffed the bills in her jeans pocket and smiled at Mrs. Ulmer. "Do you want me to come tomorrow morning? It's Saturday so I don't have school."

"Yes, I would. That will be fine. Are you going home now?"

"Yes ma'am, after I stop at the store for some dog food."

Back at the Catleton Arket she counted out the money for two cans of dog food and made some calculations. She would be able to buy a big sack of kibble in three more days. She hoped she could manage at least a twenty-five pound sack. That was the cheapest by the pound.

Right now she was so stiff and sore it was painful just carrying two cans of dog food. She was too tired to eat her snacks even though doing so would have made her backpack lighter.

The animal control truck passed her and pulled over to the curb. The lady officer waved to Cassie to come over. Cassie walked to the truck with her heart pounding.

"Hello again," said the officer. "We've had another report about that big white dog. Would you keep your eyes out for him? We don't want him to get hit by a car. If he's as big and beautiful as they say, someone would adopt him quickly. People are always looking for big guard dogs."

"Yeah, sure," said Cassie. So the officer thought her white dog would be adopted without any trouble. This should have cheered Cassie, but it didn't. She didn't want anyone else to have him. She walked slowly toward home, thinking of all the things that had happened today.

Mrs. Ulmer at first hadn't remembered hiring Cassie yesterday. But luckily she finally did. The gardening was terribly hard; Cassie had been ready to quit until she thought of watering before weeding. Worst of all, the dog catcher was still looking for the white dog. Thank goodness they hadn't found him.

She let herself in the front door and locked it as usual. She looked at her watch. It was time to feed Tokie.

Her hands hurt so much that it was hard to open the cans of dog food. She scooped the meat into the dish, painfully flattened the cans, and hid them in the box marked "cans." On top of the dog food, she put the fresh ground beef she'd saved by eating grilled cheese sandwiches the night before.

She took the dish outside and glanced at the liquidambar tree. She gasped. The white dog was there, waiting for her!

CHAPTER
10

Tokie crouched as soon as he saw Cassie, his head on his front paws, his rump in the air, his tail swinging hard back and forth. As Cassie started down the steps, he jumped up and down in wild excitement. He leaped into the air, whirled, and bounded across the yard to Cassie. He almost knocked her down.

Cassie staggered. "Down!" she exclaimed. "I've brought you your supper!" She clutched the dish tightly with both hands and hurried to the tree.

Tokie frolicked beside her and crouched again with his head on his paws, rump aloft, tail swinging, lips grinning impishly. One paw struck several times at empty air. She put the dish down quickly.

"You're *dancing!*" Cassie exclaimed. "You're doing a happy dance!" She laughed.

She retreated to the bottom step and sat down stiffly. Tokie swatted the dish onto its side and pushed around the raw ground beef before he gulped it down. As usual he sniffed at the canned dog food before he ate it. He pounced on the empty dish, shook it, tossed it in the air, and pounced on it again. Finally he licked his muzzle with his long pink tongue.

"You sure liked that fresh meat," said Cassie. "I wish you liked the canned food as much. Maybe I'll try another kind for you tomorrow."

His tail waved slowly. He suddenly dashed part way toward Cassie, stopped, crouched on his forepaws, waved one paw in the air, and bounded several steps toward the liquidambar tree. He looked over his shoulder at her.

Cassie was mystified. "What are you up to?"

Tokie repeated his performance, dashing part way toward Cassie and then starting back toward the hill behind the trees. He stopped and looked back at her, grinning.

"You want me to follow you!" Cassie suddenly exclaimed. Her whole body was aching to lie down and rest after that hour of gardening. She couldn't imagine a worse time than this for a walk. But an invitation from Tokie? It was too exciting to turn down. She painfully struggled to her feet. As soon as she started toward him, Tokie began circling, leaping, and frisking. He bounded up the hill.

"Oh, no!" moaned Cassie. There was no way she could keep up with him, but she would start out. Beyond the line of liquidambars was a rabbit path. Cassie began to climb.

She used to go hiking a lot. At first it was for the pure joy of it, the fun of being out-of-doors, away from houses and people. She had loved being out in the open, all by herself with so many rabbits and different kinds of birds to watch. And then it was because she wanted to be where she couldn't hear her mother and father arguing with each other. Before her father left, her parents argued a lot.

"I wish you'd quit fooling around with all those cars here at home," her mother had said. "Why don't you work at a regular garage like you used to?"

"I've got my business license, so it's okay to work here."

"Yes, but you'd get a regular check on time each month."

"I earn a lot more working for myself."

Cassie wondered about that. She noticed that one red car came back pretty often. The woman driver spent a lot of time talking with her father, and he hardly ever looked at the car.

The hills were always quiet and peaceful. She remembered there were three big boulders under a pine tree near the top. She'd sit and watch the ground squirrels and the rabbits going about their business as though she weren't there at all. She'd take a box of crackers or cookies with her to share with the blue jays. The jays got quite sassy, scolding her when they thought it was too long between bites.

Cassie stopped to catch her breath and scan the hill. The boulders and the pine tree were still there, but they seemed ten miles away. How had she ever climbed so far? Tokie was zigzagging across the slope, darting from one bush to another to sniff carefully and occasionally lift his leg and leave his mark. From time to time he stopped to look at her and swing his tail hard as if to cheer her on.

About a third of the way up the hill, the path went around a big white rock with a flattish top. Cassie decided if she had the strength to reach it, she would

sit there and rest and then go back down. In one place the path was awfully steep. She wrestled with the temptation to give up and go home, but then she remembered, "I didn't think you were a quitter."

Cassie muttered, "Well, I'm not," and put one foot

in front of the other. She thought about her earlier hikes and the fun of feeding the blue jays. After a while, she had been eating ten cookies for every one she gave to the blue jays.

Cassie remembered the morning she had gone into the kitchen for breakfast and her mother had told her that her dad was gone.

"Walked out of the house with a suitcase, and no, he's not coming back," said her mother, pulling out a frying pan.

"But *why?*" asked Cassie, bewildered.

Her mother banged the frying pan down so hard that Cassie jumped. "You'll have to ask him when you see him sometime."

"You mean he just took our car and drove off?" she asked cautiously.

Her mother frowned. "No, he left the car. I think somebody gave him a ride."

Cassie wondered if it was the driver of the red car, but she didn't want to ask.

Cassie reached the flat rock and carefully lowered herself onto it. Tokie came frolicking back, put his paws on the rock beside her, and gave her several huge slobbering kisses. She laughed in spite of her pain.

"I'll have to get into shape if you want me to play with you," she told him, wiping her face. Being kissed by Tokie was sort of like going through a car wash. She put her arms around him and hugged him even as he squirmed. For one brief instant, she put her face against the rough fur. He wriggled away and zoomed off again.

Cassie watched him, smiling. His funny way of trotting almost made him look like he was bicycling.

The sun dropped down behind the hill. Cassie stood up carefully. "I've got to go home now. You be good, and I'll see you tomorrow."

Tokie swung his tail and watched her start slowly down the hill. When she looked back, he was gone.

Back home she washed the dog dish. She gasped. There were tooth marks, deep ones, right into the metal, and in a couple of places his teeth had even punctured holes. It must have happened when he was playing with the dish. But how strong his jaws must be to make holes in stainless steel! She didn't know a dog could be that strong. As she started to put the dish away, she shivered a little. If her mother saw that. . . . Cassie hid the dish in the cleaning closet.

With a sack of corn chips from the cupboard, she retreated to her room and her books. Her hands were sore, her back ached, and her knees hurt, but she didn't care. Her beautiful dog was worth any amount of pain. What a wonderful creature he was, and they were truly friends.

"Hi. I'm home," said her mother's tired voice.

Reluctantly Cassie closed the book on malamutes and went into the living room, where her mother had collapsed into the brown chair. Cassie had forgotten about supper. And about TV. She had been thinking about how the white dog sniffed at the canned food before he ate it. She wondered if there were another brand of food he would like better, what he would prefer if he got to choose.

"Did you eat at work?" she asked her mother.

"No. Well, I nibbled at stuff. I guess you could fix me something."

A new thought crossed Cassie's mind. "Mom," she said. "If you could choose whatever you wanted for supper, what would you choose?"

Her mother sat bolt upright in the brown chair. "What ever made you ask that?"

"I dunno. I was just wondering. You never really get to choose anything but what they serve at Red Baron Burger."

"Yeah, you're right." Her mother rubbed her forehead. "Well, I'd like a big T-bone steak." There was a pause. "No, as long as I'm wishing, I'd wish for a giant porterhouse steak, charcoal broiled. Rare." There was a little silence. "And maybe a huge baked potato with sour cream and chives sprinkled over the top. And a little loaf of fresh baked bread on a little board with a knife to slice it, and a dish of real butter to go with it. And, oh, I don't know, some kind of special salad that they mix up right at the table in front of you. Just like at a fancy restaurant I've seen on TV." She sank back in her chair. "That's my idea of a real dinner. No fast food for me. That's what I wish."

Cassie felt a little pang. Maybe someday, years from now, she would take her mother to a fancy restaurant to eat a giant porterhouse steak, rare, and all that went with it.

She went into the kitchen and looked at the packages of ground beef in the refrigerator. Above the refrigerator were some cookbooks, and she pulled down one that said *101 Ways to Fix Hamburger.* With the book propped open to a certain page, she took out some of the ground beef and made it into two patties. She followed the recipe for cooking them, made a salad, and put the meat patties on the plates. She called her mother to the table.

"Salisbury steaks, Mom," she announced.

Her mother smiled. "Aren't we getting fancy."

Cassie shrugged and smiled. She and her mother cleaned up their plates. Ordinarily she would have made two patties for each of them, and she would have eaten all of hers and whatever her mother didn't eat. Instead, she thought happily of the ground beef still in the refrigerator. Her mother would assume it was all gone, and tomorrow Cassie could give it to Tokie. Canned food was expensive; Cassie would be glad when she could buy the dog kibble.

She rinsed the dishes, put them in the dishwasher, and went back to her room. Stretched out on her bed, she opened the book on the malamute.

Pure malamutes weren't used for sled racing because they weren't fast enough. It was the Arctic Spitz bred with other dogs that were used for racing.

Cassie frowned. There went her dream of Tokie being in the Iditarod races and then being brought to Hollywood.

She read on. The Eskimos didn't like to breed a dog with a wolf because half-breeds can be treacherous.

Cassie was startled. Tokie wasn't treacherous. He was just lonely. If he had any wolf in him, it was only a little bit.

C H A P T E R
11

On Saturday morning Cassie ate breakfast and left
for the Ulmers' while her mother was still asleep.

As she rang the doorbell she wondered, What will
happen this time?

The door opened, and Mrs. Ulmer stared at Cassie
a minute.

"I remember you," she said. "You've come to work
on the lawn."

"Right!" said Cassie, relieved.

"Your name is Cassandra."

"Right again," said Cassie, smiling.

Mrs. Ulmer went with her into the garage and
pointed toward the back. "There's the bench for
kneeling I told you about, the garden gloves, and
the gardening tools. Help yourself to what you need.
Just be sure to put everything back the way you
found it. I can't find things if they're not where they
belong."

At the back of the garage, Cassie discovered
a work table littered with tools and some garden
gloves. She poked around and underneath the work
table found the bench for kneeling stuck inside a
child's red wagon. She dragged the red wagon out

released the kneeling bench. The wagon was
ᴗnd rusty. Faintly visible was the name FLYER
painted on the side. It must have belonged to one
of their kids, Cassie thought, and she shoved it back
under the work table.

She didn't need the kneeling bench. Her watering
yesterday had really paid off. Her hands were still
quite sore, but she wore the heaviest pair of garden
gloves and had no trouble at all digging up the rest
of the weeds in Square One. Then she tackled Square
Two.

After a while, she rocked back on her heels and
studied the lawn. It really was looking better. She
decided to take a break and eat one of her snacks—
a packet of crackers spread with peanut butter. She
sat down cross-legged.

Mrs. Ulmer silently appeared beside her. Cassie
jumped.

"Would you like some cider to go with your
snack?"

"Oh, that would be great. Please." Cassie got up
and brushed off her jeans. She laid down the gloves
and trowel and followed Mrs. Ulmer onto the porch.
She looked down at her shoes. "I'm too dirty to go in
the house. I'll just sit here on the steps."

Mrs. Ulmer nodded approval. She came back and
handed Cassie a tall glass of cider. "You're as good
a worker as you said you were. Are you like this with
all your jobs?"

Cassie took a long drink, stared at the cider, and
shook her head. "No, only when I'm really interested."

Mrs. Ulmer laughed. "So. You do like gardening."

"Yes ma'am. I used to keep our lawn and the shrubbery real nice, but when Mom started working, I had to do more inside the house, and I sort of let the outside go."

"That's understandable."

On the porch was a dilapidated folding chair. Mrs. Ulmer pulled it over next to Cassie and sat down. "Tell me about your dog. What color is he?" she asked.

Cassie started smiling. "He's white. Pure white. He shines like silver—and yesterday he was waiting for me! When I went outside to feed him, he was already there, and he did a sort of happy dance to show how glad he was to see me. He almost knocked me down."

"I wish I had seen that!"

"And after he cleaned up his dish, he acted like he wanted me to go for a walk, so I did, up the hill."

"My, my. It looks like your dog has adopted you, just as you hoped."

Cassie nodded. "It sure was hard climbing that hill, but I didn't want to disappoint him. I went about a third of the way up. It's a steep hill."

"He's certainly lucky you found him. What's his name?"

"I call him Tokie, short for Toklata. I got that from a book about Alaska."

"Why Alaska?"

"Oh, I forgot to tell you. He looks like a sled dog from Alaska, with slanty eyes and thick fur."

"Goodness! A Siberian husky, perhaps?"

"A husky is too small. My dog is even taller than a malamute. I can't find any pictures that look just like him. My science teacher says he's probably a cross-breed. They do that a lot with sled dogs." She stood up and handed the empty glass to Mrs. Ulmer. "Thanks. I've got to get back to work."

"It's unusual for an Alaskan sled dog to be running around loose, don't you think?"

Cassie hesitated. "Well, I think somebody brought him down here from Alaska, and he jumped out of their car and they don't know where they lost him."

"You're looking in the lost and found ads, aren't you?"

"Mr. Crowell keeps looking in the paper for me, but whoever owns him hasn't advertised."

"Why don't *you* advertise in the paper?"

Cassie scuffed the dirt with one foot while she thought about that. "I don't want to. He was so scared when I found him that I'll bet somebody has mistreated him. Why should I send him back to people like that?"

"Because he belongs to them, that's why," Mrs. Ulmer answered.

Cassie looked at her without blinking. "I'll think about it." She went to work on the weeds, jabbing each one as hard as if it had been the person who had mistreated her white dog.

Mrs. Ulmer watched her for several minutes. "You can work for two hours today if it's not too much for you," she said.

"I'll be glad to," said Cassie. That meant she could

buy a big sack of dog kibble today, for sure. "Say, I saw a little red wagon under the work table. Could I borrow it to haul a big sack of dog kibble home?"

"Of course," Mrs. Ulmer replied. "I use it for hauling flower pots around. It belonged to our son Danny when he was little. You can take it home with you when you leave and bring it back on Monday."

Cassie saved the last half hour for watering the different squares of lawn. She coiled up the hose, put back the gardening tools, and pulled the little red wagon out of the garage. It squeaked terribly as it wobbled along behind her. Mrs. Ulmer smiled and handed Cassie eight dollars.

"Sounds like it needs some oil."

"I'll find some at home," she said. The noise of the wagon kept time with her steps as she trudged off to the Catleton Arket.

"What in the world you got there?" asked the clerk as Cassie pulled the wagon inside the door.

"I've come to buy a sack of dog kibble, and I'll haul it home in the wagon." She pulled it to the back of the store where the kibble was stacked. "And I need a can of dog food."

Mr. Ulmer was at the cash register and watched her progress. "Looks like our wagon," he commented.

"It is," said Cassie. "Mrs. Ulmer loaned it to me for the dog biscuit."

"It sure needs some oil." He brought out a spray can from under the counter and bent over the wheels. He twirled each one in turn. "That ought to do it."

"Gee, thanks," said Cassie, moving the wagon back and forth. The noise was gone.

"Anyone who works hard like you do for a dog deserves help. And how is your dog?"

"He's fine," replied Cassie. "Yesterday we went for a walk together. We climbed partway up the hill."

The clerk asked, "You want a forty-pounder, chunk?"

"Chunk?"

"Chunk's for big dogs, and that's what you got."

"Yes, chunk," she said.

"Thought so." He lifted down a large sack of kibble and laid it in the wagon. Near the sacks of dog kibble hung some leashes and collars and assorted toys for dogs. Cassie studied them. She thought about getting a collar for Tokie but decided to wait until they were really good friends before she tried to put one on him.

She looked at the toys. A squeaky mouse with a fierce expression caught her eye. She handed it to the clerk. "I'll take this, too."

She paid Mr. Ulmer and started home, pulling the heavy wagon behind her.

When she came to Miss Kimura's house, she saw the beautiful gold-colored Lexus on the driveway.

At least she doesn't work on Saturday, thought Cassie. Where did she work? she wondered. As she walked by, Miss Kimura came out of her front door and called, "Come up on the porch for a couple of minutes, would you? I'd like to talk to you."

Cassie hesitated, then parked the wagon and went up the walk. Miss Kimura motioned to one of the two patio chairs for Cassie and sat down in the other.

"You saw my gardener the other day. He's good at gardening, but he drives me crazy with that leaf-blower machine. It's so noisy, I can't work at all when it's running."

"What kind of work do you do?"

"I'd like someone to rake those sycamore leaves by hand. I'll pay you five dollars an hour. Would you be interested?"

C H A P T E R
12

"Rake your leaves by hand? Sure," said Cassie, recovering from her astonishment at the unexpected offer. She grinned. "I can do that, as long as Saturday is okay. I work at Mrs. Ulmer's every day after school." Cassie began planning all the things she could do for her dog with the extra money.

Miss Kimura smiled.

"Can you start next Saturday?"

"You bet," said Cassie. She went down the walk and trudged on home, pulling the little red wagon with the dog food. Miss Kimura was really nice. Cassie remembered her mother frowning whenever Miss Kimura's name was mentioned. She couldn't imagine why her mother didn't like her. Usually her mother got along well with everybody. Except with Cassie.

Once home, Cassie faced a new problem. Where could she hide the dog food so her mother wouldn't find it—and neither would a neighbor's dog if one should get loose? Certainly not in the garage. Maybe in the cleaning closet, behind the vacuum cleaner and the laundry soap. Her mom depended on Cassie to do the vacuuming and the laundry.

She struggled with the sack of dog food, wrestled it up the back steps, and dragged it over to the closet. By shifting around the cleaning things and the big box of laundry soap, she worked the sack of dog biscuit behind the vacuum cleaner. An old dust cloth gave her an idea. When it was carefully draped part way over the sack, she stepped back and examined the result. Even if her mom did look, she wouldn't see anything unusual.

She almost forgot about the little red wagon. She went outside and surveyed their yard. Finally she pushed the little red wagon under the porch, as far back under the steps as she could reach. There was no reason at all for her mother to look there.

It wasn't quite time for lunch, but she was hungry from working in the garden. She looked in the refrigerator. There wasn't much to choose from because it was getting toward the end of the week. It was about time for her mom to go marketing. She always went on one of her days off.

On her plate, Cassie put a large dill pickle and slices from the tomato in the refrigerator. Quickly she made a sandwich of cold cuts with the last of the baloney and the cheese. A sack of potato chips was almost empty, but there were a few chips in the bottom. She put it beside her plate. A tall glass of milk finished her preparations for lunch. She sat down at the kitchen table and happily thought about the ground beef left over from the Salisbury steaks last night.

There was about half a pound. She'd give that to

Tokie along with the can of food and several cups of dog kibble. Thank goodness she had bought the sack of kibble for him. He certainly ate a lot, but now he could eat all he wanted. It wouldn't surprise her if the dog's owners had decided it was just too expensive to keep him, and when he ran away, they didn't want him back.

She propped open the book on Alaska that Mr. Crowell had gotten for her and began to read, eating absentmindedly as she read.

The book was about remote Eskimo tribes that depended on hunting for a living and consequently on their sled dogs to help them hunt and pack the game. There were lots of photographs of Eskimos hunting, of the dogs carrying huge packs trotting alongside the hunters, and of Eskimos driving dog sleds over uneven ground and across great ice fields.

There were even diagrams of the three different ways to hitch dog teams to sleds. She wondered if she could put a harness on Tokie and have him haul his own dog kibble home in the little red wagon. She smiled as she thought of how that would look and what the neighbors would say.

But none of the sled dogs looked like Tokie.

She read on. The faster she read, the more slowly she ate. She finally stopped eating.

She was fascinated by the pictures of the sled dogs curled up asleep under huge snow drifts, their noses tucked under their tails, oblivious to the storms raging above them. Even at forty below zero, the dogs were comfortable sleeping outdoors. Cassie shook her head. It would really be hard to keep Tokie cool next summer.

The book told of the ways in which malamutes and wolves looked alike and the ways in which they were different. The malamute's tail curled up over his back; a wolf's usually hung straight down. The malamute was stocky and very strong, good for packing and hauling heavy sleds; a wolf was strong also, but he was tall and thin.

Malamutes had dark eyes; wolves had yellow eyes.

She turned the page and drew in her breath sharply. There, unmistakably, was a photograph of her white dog! Two white dogs, both exactly like Tokie! Each had a large head with a long narrow muzzle, slanted almond eyes, a big ruff of fur around his neck, long thin legs, huge feet, and a heavy brush of tail.

Underneath the photograph was the caption: "Canis lupus Arctos—two Arctic wolves from Ellesmere Island."

Cassie stared. A wolf? She had suspected Tokie could have a little bit of wolf in him, but to *be* a real wolf? An Arctic wolf? A shiver ran down her spine.

She read over again the paragraphs explaining the differences between sled dogs and wolves. The wolf's description was exactly like Tokie's except for one thing. The sled dog's eyes are always dark; a wolf's eyes are yellow. Cassie suddenly realized that Tokie had never quite looked her full in the face;

she had always assumed his eyes were brown. But were they? She determined that when she gave him his dinner, she would look him squarely in the eye.

Cassie hardly remembered how the rest of the afternoon passed. She read on, her food untouched, the TV silent, until she realized with a start that it was nearly feeding time. She emptied the new can of dog food into the metal dish, added the fresh ground beef, and poured a generous heap of dog kibble over it. She went outside, holding the dog dish firmly, determined to act just as she had the day before.

Tokie was waiting for her and went into his happy dance, as if seeing her were more important than eating. She put the dish down by the tree and re-treated to the steps. The dog glanced once at the dish but finished his happy dance, spun around as if for joy, and raced across the yard to the steps. He hurled himself upon Cassie and slobbered kisses on her face, his eyes almost closed in his lopsided impish grin.

His description might fit that of a wolf, but he didn't act like she thought wolves should act. Right now he was acting just like a dog. There must be some mistake. Cassie, relieved, put her arms around him and hugged him. At that moment, he drew back and twisted his head around and gazed into her face.

His eyes were not the trusting brown of a dog's; they were deep pools of yellow sunlight.

Cassie was sure of it now. Her dog with the golden eyes was a wolf.

CHAPTER
13

Stunned, Cassie sat stock still. She had always read that wolves were bloodthirsty. Maybe some wolves were, but if Toklata were a real wolf, he certainly wasn't bloodthirsty. He was lonely.

Tokie gave her another slobbering kiss and went to his dish. He put one big paw on the edge and tipped it over. The dog kibble and the meat shot all over the ground. He sniffed long and hard at the kibble and glanced sideways at Cassie. He crouched down on his front legs, lay down completely, and rolled over on the kibble. In obvious delight, he wriggled back and forth over the dog biscuit while his tail thrashed the ground.

Cassie stared. "You're supposed to *eat* that, you rascal, you!" Tokie finally stood up, shook himself hard, and to Cassie's horror, lifted his leg and peed over as much of the dog kibble as he could. Cassie was speechless with frustration.

"After all I've done for you!" she said. Toklata glanced at her, grinned, swung his tail, and went to the meat.

He pushed the ground beef around before gulping it down, and last of all he ate the canned dog food.

He licked his chops, wrinkled his nose at the dog kibble, and faced her. His tail swung, and then he crouched, inviting her for a walk.

Cassie was still in a state of shock from her discovery. She watched him in a daze. She suddenly realized the dry dog food was completely wasted.

"Oh no!" she exclaimed. "You're supposed to eat the dog kibble. You've *got* to eat the dog kibble. I bought it for you so you'd have enough to eat. I can't afford to feed you just meat."

Toklata swung his tail back and forth and frisked in circles, scattering the dog kibble.

"*What* am I going to *do?*" she said.

Tokie waved his tail harder, crouched, and gave her his funny lopsided grin. Was he laughing at her?

He suddenly bounded toward the hill, looking back at her. Cassie shivered. Was she supposed to go walking with a *wolf*?

She was sure there weren't any more wild wolves in California. But the scientific part of her mind said, "You are friends with an Arctic wolf. How did he get here?" Tokie's being a wolf explained a lot of things, like the size of his teeth and the strength of his jaws—making holes in the stainless-steel dish.

She had read that people could keep wolves for projects like making movies, so maybe he was one of those. But being a wolf was the real reason he was slow to make friends. He hadn't been mistreated; he just wasn't a dog.

She stood up, and Tokie started up the hill toward

the rabbit path. He looked over his shoulder, waved his tail, and bounded ahead.

Okay, so he's a wolf, Cassie thought. Just because she hadn't known before that he was a wolf and now she did know didn't make any difference in their being friends, did it? What you name an animal doesn't matter; it's how you feel about each other.

Elation ran through her like electricity. No matter what he was, she and Tokie were truly friends.

She marched up the path, keeping her eyes on the wolf. He zigzagged across the hill ahead of her, now hesitating at certain bushes to sniff and lift his leg and pee, now stopping abruptly to examine an invisible something of importance, then dashing off.

She reached the flat rock and collapsed. When Tokie bounded to her side and almost pushed her over with affection, she laughed and ran her fingers through his rough coat. Imagine me, she thought, Cassandra Beasley, friends with a wolf. The most beautiful white wolf in the world. She had a lot to learn about wolves and what they were really like. She needed to know how to take care of a wolf.

Tokie leaned against her and then dropped down at her feet, thumped his tail, yawned (oh those enormous teeth), and stretched out beside her. He wriggled partly onto his back with his legs up in the air, his huge paws dangling. The size of his feet was out of proportion to the rest of him. Cassie giggled. She ran her fingers back and forth over his stomach, and he whined and squeaked with pleasure.

The light was fading. Where does he spend the night? Cassie wondered. Every evening it was getting dark earlier.

Suddenly she remembered that her mother would be coming home. Reluctantly she stood up and pushed Tokie with one foot.

"Time to go," she announced, stretching.

He understood. He rolled over and stood up, staring into the distance. He trotted off in his strange, bicycling gait, looked back at her once and waved his tail, and then disappeared around the side of the hill.

"Good night," Cassie said in a low voice. "See you tomorrow."

She followed the rabbit path down the hill, still in a glow from her discovery. She was thinking hard.

She knew there were regulations about keeping exotic animals like lions and tigers outside a zoo. There must be regulations about keeping wolves because wolves are wild animals, too. But maybe she could keep Tokie as a pet and not tell anybody he was a wolf. She wondered how long she could get away with it. Then a dreadful thought struck her.

How would she feel if Tokie were *her* wolf and she had lost him? Whoever owned the wolf would miss him a lot and would certainly want him back.

Cassie sighed. She would have to find out where he came from and give him back to his owner before animal control found him. She knew she had to do it. She had found a wolf, but she had lost her dog. She could never take him to the vet's for shots, or put a collar on him, or get a license for him.

Her mind raced on. The big white dog had already been reported to animal control. Now that he was coming every day to her yard, suppose someone saw him who realized he was a wolf? What would they do? Probably call the police. She could only hope whoever saw him wouldn't know he was a wolf. Like Cassie, the neighbor might think he was a sled dog.

Cassie wondered what the animal control officer would think if she found out the animal she was looking for was really an Arctic wolf.

When Cassie reached their yard, she got a rake out of the garage and gathered into a pile the chunks of spilled dog kibble, which had started to dissolve where Tokie had peed on them. She managed to get most of the kibble in the dust pan. She shuddered as she examined again the teeth marks in the metal dish. She should have known a dog couldn't do that to a steel dish. She poured the kibble into the garbage can, washed the dustpan and the dish, and hid them in the closet.

What was she going to do with forty pounds of dog kibble if Tokie wouldn't eat it? If she didn't give him any meat but just the kibble, would he eat the kibble? What if he wouldn't eat it and decided never to come back?

Cassie went into her room and lay down on her bed, thinking. Tokie had to belong to someone, somewhere.

If there had been anything in the papers about a wolf, Mr. Crowell would have noticed. Maybe Tokie had escaped from the compound while they were training him for the movies, and they didn't want people to know there was a wolf on the loose, even while they were looking for him.

Maybe the best thing would be for her to advertise in the paper for Tokie's owner, like Mrs. Ulmer had suggested. Mrs. Ulmer would like that. Cassie would write the ad as though she had found just a white dog and would ask whoever answered it to give a complete description of him. His real owner would describe a wolf, even if the owner didn't say that's what he was. She couldn't give Tokie to anybody but his real owner.

But not yet, she said to herself. Tokie was her friend. Right now she wanted most of all the chance to enjoy him, to learn more about wolves. It could be a great science project for her!

She could see the kids in her science class staring at her in admiration. Lindsay would be sorry she had stopped being friends with Cassie for Shannon and Joanna. And Shannon and Joanna would want to be her friends, too. They would ask her, "What's it like, having a wolf for a pet?" She and Lindsay would hang out together again and talk on the phone for hours.

Cassie didn't hear the front door open and close.

"Hi, I'm home," said her mother's voice. It didn't sound tired at all. Cassie went into the living room.

Her mother was standing up straight in her uniform, smiling.

"Hi, Mom. What's up?" asked Cassie, watching her mother's face. Her mother somehow looked younger.

"You don't need to fix me anything to eat. I'm going out for dinner. I came home to change."

"Going out? Who with?" Once in a while her mother and several of the other women (her mother always called them "the girls") at the Red Baron Burger went to a movie or someplace together. But this seemed different.

Her mother shrugged. "Somebody I met at work." She went into her bedroom and shut the door.

Cassie felt uneasy. She stood outside the door, cleared her throat, and asked, "Is it a man?"

There was a silence and, finally, "Yes. It's a man, but don't worry. He's very nice."

Cassie felt a shock. Twice she started to say something, but couldn't. Then she squared her shoulders and said boldly, "But Mom, aren't you still married to Dad?"

CHAPTER
14

Another silence. An exasperated voice came through the door. "Yes, but for heaven's sake, this is just business." Her mother came out, wearing her robe. "You don't expect me to be a hermit just because your father ran off someplace, do you?" Her mother went in the bathroom and turned on the shower.

Actually I do, thought Cassie. Her mom wasn't supposed to go out with anybody as long as she was still married to her father. Nobody had said anything about a divorce. Not yet.

After a while, her mother went back to her room.

Cassie clenched her teeth and sat down on the sofa. She couldn't believe how absolutely awful and unfair life was. She felt as though the whole world was coming down on her.

First her best friend left her to hang out with two girls she hated. Worse, her father deserted their family. He wasn't the kind of man who hugged or kissed or mentioned love, but Cassie knew he loved her. And then he left. Her parents hadn't been yelling at each other for a while, just being real silent when they were together, and then, out of the clear blue sky, he left. And he didn't say good-bye to Cassie. She couldn't understand how he could do that to her.

Her mother didn't cry at all; she just kept slamming doors and looking awfully mad. Cassie didn't cry either, not for a long time. She felt numb.

Then today she lost the beautiful white dog with the golden eyes. She had been counting on adopting him without saying anything to her mother. Once her mother found out that Cassie was supporting him and had been taking care of him for a long time, her mother would have to give in and say yes. She would come home from school and find him wagging his tail and barking a welcome and she would hug him and he would lick her face and they would romp together. Today she found out he was somebody's wolf, and that she must try to give him back to his owner.

And now it seemed as if she was losing her mother. Just as she and her mother were beginning to get along together. She'd stopped hassling Cassie about eating too much and not having any friends and not getting good grades when she was smart enough to get them. And now her mother had found a man, a jerk who asked a married woman to go out with him. That was okay in soap operas but not in real life. Not with *her* mother.

Her mother and dad would divorce and her mother would marry this jerk. That would make him Cassie's stepfather.

She hunched over and watched the brown chair

blur through her tears. Life wasn't fair at all. It was rotten. There were too many problems and no solutions to any of them. There was no way out. Two kids in her school had run away this past year, and a third one had committed suicide. Cassie had always wondered how kids could do such a thing, but for the first time, she thought she knew.

Her mother came out of her room wearing high heels and a green print dress with a slim skirt and a bow tied at the neck. Her face was kind of pink, and she wore deep pink lipstick, and her brown hair was brushed out so it sort of floated around her shoulders. Cassie hated to admit it, but her mother looked pretty. She hadn't looked like that for a long time.

Her mother put her coat over one arm. "Don't forget to turn off the TV. I'm not sure when I'll be home, but it won't be late."

I bet, said Cassie to herself. She felt angry. And jealous. Her mother was going to have dinner, maybe at a fancy restaurant, and Cassie wasn't the one taking her there. As her mother walked out the door, Cassie said suddenly, "Good grief, isn't he even going to pick you up?"

Her mother shook her head quickly. "No, I'm meeting him downtown. I thought it would be better. G'night, dear." The door closed.

Why? thought Cassie. What was she ashamed of? Their house? Her? She wouldn't be surprised. For a long time she had wondered if that was the real reason her father had left.

She chewed on her lower lip. If her parents were
that ashamed of her, they'd be glad if she left, but
where would she go? She couldn't disappear into
the city; she hated the city. She could run off into the

country and maybe get a job on a farm, cooking or doing housework. But a city girl like her would be conspicuous. Soon there would be questions.

She certainly didn't want to think about suicide. If she did try it, she would probably mess it up, like everything else she did. She could see herself climbing onto the kitchen stool with the clothesline in a noose around her neck, kicking away the stool, and the line breaking or the knot coming undone. She'd end up in the hospital with a broken leg. With the way her life was going, both legs.

And then the vision of the Arctic wolf with the golden eyes flashed before her. That beautiful Arctic wolf who was her friend. What would become of him if she weren't there to feed him and to see that he got back to his owner? What in the world was she thinking of?

"I didn't think you were a quitter," she heard Mrs. Ulmer say, and Cassie rose to her feet. She remembered how Mrs. Ulmer's voice had wavered when she talked about having to put her dog to sleep—that lady was really tender hearted. And how would Mrs. Ulmer feel when no one showed up to finish working on her lawn and her garden? Mrs. Ulmer and the Arctic wolf were counting on her.

She definitely couldn't run away. She had to figure out some kind of a solution for herself.

Her father had taught her to make a plan when something was wrong, starting with the simplest thing first to try to fix it. She remembered the day he had motioned to a white Chevy coupe in their garage.

"The owner brought in this car because he got tired of having to jump-start it. He says he's sure it's the alternator." He had the hood up and waved a hand at the engine. "Maybe, but alternators are expensive. Always start with the simplest thing. I look first at the battery." He pointed. "See how corroded the terminals are?"

"Yuck," said Cassie. She made a face at the white goop collected around the wires.

"So I'm going to clean them up and try to start it."

In twenty minutes, the motor turned over nicely and began humming away. Her father grinned at her.

"Wow!" said Cassie. "I'll bet not having to buy a new whatcha-ma-callit saved him a bunch of time and money."

Her father would want her to make a plan.

She couldn't do anything about her father's leaving, or about her mother's new friend—at least not yet. The most important thing was to find the owner of her wolf. Mrs. Ulmer had said she could put an ad in the paper.

She looked up Mrs. Ulmer's phone number and dialed it carefully. When the soft voice answered Cassie said, "It's me—Cassie, Mrs. Ulmer."

"Who?" said Mrs. Ulmer.

Cassie took a deep breath. "I work in your yard every day. I water your lawn and then weed it. My name is Cassie."

Silence. "Oh. Oh, yes. What can I do for you?"

"I guess I'd better put an ad in the paper for the owner of the white dog that came into our yard. What do I do?"

"Oh yes. I remember. You're a brave girl. Just a minute and I'll look up the phone number for you."

Cassie copied it on the pad beside the telephone. "What if somebody answers who isn't his real owner but who just wants a white dog?"

"Maybe you'd better take out a box number instead of giving your address. They'll have to write, and you'll be able to tell from the letter whether or not they're the owner."

"What's a box number?"

"Some people don't want their phone number or address in the paper, so the newspaper lets them use a box number. The replies go to the newspaper, and you pick them up there. How would you like *me* to take out a box number, and I'll give any letters to you? Mr. Ulmer could pick them up when he goes in to get the mail for the grocery store. That way no one would be able to trace the dog to your house and kidnap him. Dognap him."

Cassie smiled faintly. "That would be awfully nice, Mrs. Ulmer. I'll pay you for the ad."

"Not necessary. The paper runs three-line 'found' ads for three days for free. I'll be glad to pay for the cost of the box number because you're doing what's right, and that's what counts. What do you want the ad to say?"

"Beautiful big white dog found October 15th in . . ." She hesitated and then named their town, "in Altadena." She added, "Owner must give complete description before claiming."

"Very good. I'll take care of it tomorrow when I get home from church. It will be in Monday's paper."

"Thanks a lot." She tried to sound cheerful. She was on the right track, and she didn't have to worry about someone who didn't really own him coming to her house to get Tokie.

Until the owner showed up, she was going to have a good time with her wolf. She would read all about wolves in the library. She would go for walks with him and write up notes about his behavior for her science class.

And then she thought, what if the owner never sees the ad and never shows up? She groaned. Maybe Mr. Crowell would know what to do. She could tell him the truth. But until that happened, she wouldn't tell *anyone* that Tokie was a wolf.

CHAPTER
15

Cassie awoke Sunday morning knowing that something momentous had happened the day before. She remembered: Toklata. Her dog with the golden eyes was an Arctic wolf. Cassie's heart thudded inside her chest.

And another thing: Her mother had gone on a date last night. Cassie had tried to stay awake until her mother got home, but she'd fallen sound asleep and had slept the night through. She looked at her watch. Her mother must already have left for work.

Cassie rolled over in bed and put her face in her pillow. Her only cheerful thought was that she didn't have to go to school or to work at Mrs. Ulmer's.

On second thought, she wished she could go to the Ulmers'; it was funny, but punching out weeds was very satisfying. She decided to work in their own yard. And later she'd go for another walk with Tokie. She climbed out of bed.

She wondered if her mother had had a good time last night. She hoped that she hadn't. That guy must be a con artist to get her mother to go out with him when she was still married to her father. Her mother wasn't the kind of person who'd lie about that.

Cassie would find out more when her mother got home from work.

Suddenly she remembered that her mother would have Monday and Tuesday off. Her mother worked on Saturdays, so she got two days off in a row. What a pain. If her mother were home all day tomorrow, how could Cassie take back the little red wagon and stay to work at the Ulmers'? Or feed Tokie and go for a walk with him? As much as Cassie disliked the idea, if her mother's new friend took her away somewhere, it would help a lot. Cassie immediately felt disloyal to her father and pushed the idea aside.

She dressed in her gardening clothes, ate a sort of brunch, and went to work in their front yard. She pulled out all the dead plants in the flower bed, spaded the dirt, and turned on the sprinklers. Mrs. Ulmer was going to have her plant chrysanthemums in their garden when Cassie got all the weeds pulled up and the garden spaded.

Afterward she attacked her homework. Usually she did as little as possible on English and history, but Mrs. Ulmer's words kept taunting her. "I didn't know you were a quitter." She chewed the end of her pencil and worked carefully on each of the assignments. Eventually she turned off the sprinklers and then returned to her math.

With a start she looked at her watch. How fast the day had gone! She had worked through lunch, and now it was almost time to feed Tokie.

She decided to try feeding Tokie the dog kibble one more time. She put some ground beef in his dish, covered it with kibble, and set the dish behind the liquidambar tree. She was going to move it farther away each day so eventually she could feed him behind the garage and no one would see him at all. She sat down on the steps.

A few minutes later, Tokie appeared and sniffed the dish. With one big paw he tipped it over, scattering meat and kibble in all directions.

"Not again!" exclaimed Cassie.

Tokie ate the meat, dirty as it was, and pawed the kibble around. He lay down on it and wriggled as before. Cassie wondered if he would pee on it as he had yesterday. She couldn't think of any way to keep him from it if that's what he wanted to do. He did, and Cassie groaned.

Then he went back to the bowl, scrubbed it with his tongue, licked his muzzle, swung his tail back and forth, and crouched as an invitation for a walk.

Cassie sighed. "What am I going to do with you if you won't eat the kibble?" Tokie wrinkled up his lips in a grin and swung his tail harder. His "Come ON!" was as clear to understand as anything. Cassie hitched up her jeans and followed him past the trees and up the rabbit path.

She glanced up the hill to see Tokie suddenly freeze midstride, crouch low, and begin creeping stealthily forward. Ten yards away was a rabbit, ears back and cheeks and whiskers quivering as it bent over to nibble a tiny green plant.

"Please don't!" exclaimed Cassie, guessing what

would happen next. Tokie leaped up and sprang on the rabbit so quickly it never knew what had happened. Cassie heard a single squeak, and Tokie shook the limp form. He bounded up the hill with the dead rabbit in his mouth. Cassie, trembling, looked away. She hesitated for a long minute and finally, keeping her eyes on the path in front of her, continued her climb to the flat white rock. She sat down and stole a quick look at Tokie. He was crouching over the rabbit and devouring it systematically. Dogs kill rabbits and hardly ever eat them, she told herself. This is fresh meat, better for him than canned dog food.

While she watched, fascinated and revolted at the same time, he ate every part of the rabbit—the insides, the head and ears, the legs, crunching up all the bones, and finally every bit of fur. Cassie felt faint. She lifted her eyes to the pine trees at the top of the hill. To her surprise, they didn't look nearly as far away as they had the first day.

Maybe next week I'll hike all the way up, she thought. As long as I still have Tokie. His eating the rabbit had depressed her, but the thought of losing her beautiful white friend almost plunged her into despair.

In a crevice of the white rock lay a blue-bellied lizard. His tiny throat was pulsing with fright as though it were his heart. She had read that wolves ate lizards. "Run and hide," she said softly. The lizard flicked his tail and disappeared.

She took a deep breath of the fragrant air, faintly

pungent with grass and sage and pine. She had forgotten how good it smelled up here.

If only there were some kind of job where she could work with animals when she grew up, Cassie thought. Not as a veterinarian, and not as a zoo keeper, but instead in a job where she could work *among* animals, in the wild, out in the woods, or wherever they lived. Helping the animals, putting them back together, like she had told Mrs. Ulmer. She remembered how Mrs. Ulmer had smiled at that.

Tokie zigzagged across the hillside. Cassie looked; not even a scrap of fur remained of the rabbit. The wolf came bounding back to her, put his paws on the rock, and tried to lick her face. Cassie turned her face away but hugged him just the same. Seeing him kill the rabbit had almost made her sick, but what should she expect of a wolf?

Tokie suddenly took her right arm in his jaws and shook it playfully while he leered at her out of the corner of his eyes. Even though he was gentle, she could feel the incredible strength of his jaws. She held her breath. He let go of her arm, and with a sigh he flopped down at her feet as though he were a faithful dog. Cassie rubbed the teeth marks on her arm. "Whew," she said. Maybe keeping a wolf around wasn't entirely a great idea.

The sun disappeared behind the hill, and Cassie leaned over to pat Tokie. "Time to go, my friend," she said. He rose and stretched and yawned, and as Cassie got to her feet, he trotted out of sight in his funny swinging gait. "See you," she said, and made her way back down the hill.

She was reading one of the books on Alaska when she heard her mother's voice. "Hi, I'm home." Hastily Cassie put down the book, but she made herself stroll into the living room.

"Did you have a good time last night?"

Her mother looked uncertain. "Yes, sure. We went to the Candlelight Inn. The food was awfully good."

"Are you going out with him again?"

Her mother hesitated. "Maybe later on, but not tomorrow. It's my first day off, and I have a lot of catching up to do—laundry and marketing and stuff. Then I think I'd like to sit around and do nothing for a while."

That spelled disaster for Cassie. The idea she'd pushed away wriggled back into her head—why not use her mother's new man friend to keep her mother busy while Tokie was around?

"Listen, Mom," Cassie said casually, "I'll clean the living room, so next time you can have your friend come in."

Her mother looked up. "You don't have to do that. I'm not going to ask him in."

Cassie shrugged. "Does your friend like movies? You haven't been to the movies in ages. Why don't you get him to take you to a show? There are some really good ones on."

Her mother looked puzzled. "You've changed your mind. Yesterday you weren't happy about my having dinner with him."

"Yeah, but I got to thinking. You work so hard, you ought to have some fun once in a while."

Her mother smiled. "I'm glad you feel that way. He does want to see me again, but it's not a real date."

"That's nice, Mom," Cassie said, faking a happy voice. "Can I fix you something to eat?"

"A little. I ate a lot last night. It was great."

Cassie went into the kitchen and thumbed through *101 Ways to Fix Hamburger.* There was a lemon in the fruit bin, so she decided on Lemon Dumplings with Ground Beef. That way she could fix a big meal without using much meat. She measured some biscuit mix into a bowl and went to work.

At the table her mother looked up once and remarked, "This is really good," but the rest of the time she ate as though she were thinking about her date last night.

CHAPTER
16

After dinner, her mother sat in the living room, humming to herself.

"Mom, what's your friend's name and where does he live?"

"Is this the third degree?" asked her mother. She suddenly smiled. "His name is Fred Schirmeyer. He lives in Ventura." She hesitated. "Well, I am planning to meet him again. Later on this week. Just dinner somewhere."

Cassie thought, If he lives in Ventura, what's he doing over here? Ventura is miles away, over on the coast.

Her mother got up and smiled at Cassie. "You're getting to be a very good cook. It's too bad you can't go with me to help with the marketing tomorrow morning."

Cassie shrugged. "Yeah, it would be nice." She was still worried about tomorrow. She didn't want to give up feeding Tokie and taking a walk with him. "Listen, Mom. If you're starting to go out with a guy, why don't you go shopping tomorrow afternoon for something to wear? There are lots of neat shops in the mall."

Her mother stood in the doorway a minute. "I've got some nice clothes I haven't worn for ages."

"Yeah, but they're probably out of style. You could use something new, couldn't you?"

A smile flickered over her mother's face. "Yes, I probably could," she said. "That's a good idea. I'll market first and then go shopping. I'll have my charge card ready."

Cassie knew her mother. The shopping would easily last all afternoon until late. Tomorrow Cassie could take the little red wagon back to the Ulmers' after school, do the gardening, feed Tokie, and even have a walk with her wolf before her mother came home.

The next day as soon as Cassie walked into the science room, she saw Brad in the center of a group of admiring kids.

"What's up?" Cassie asked one of the students.

"He shot a deer Saturday, a five-point buck. He got it on his first shot. He's telling us all about it."

Joe Pinatelli joined the group. He said, "Where do you go to practice shooting?"

Brad laughed. "My dad goes to the gun club in town to practice, but he says I don't need to because I'm a natural. He says I'm a crack shot—got a really good eye for it. I can even get a rabbit when he's running." He grinned. "Man, now that is really cool. I put my sights on that bunny as he's tearing past, follow him till I've got his speed, move my gun ahead of where he's going, and pull the trigger. Bingo!"

He looked around at the admiring group. "Just call me Keeler the Killer."

Cassie shivered and went to her seat.

Mr. Crowell asked Cassie to see him after class. "This morning's paper had an ad asking for the owner of a big white dog. Is that yours?"

Cassie nodded. "Mrs. Ulmer put it in for me. She said I should use a box number so no one could dog-nap my dog."

Mr. Crowell smiled. "That was a good idea."

"I didn't really want to, but. . . ." She shrugged and handed him the two library books. "These were great. Thanks a lot."

Mr. Crowell put them on his desk and handed her another book. "You might like this one, too."

Cassie jumped and drew back her hand. The title was *Of Wolves and Men.* "What's this for?" she demanded.

"You said he's probably a sled dog, and some of the sled dogs are wolflike. I thought you might be interested in learning something about wolves."

"Oh." She took the book. "Yeah, I guess I could." She smiled as innocently as possible and put it in her backpack. She was lucky. Mr. Crowell hadn't really guessed at all, and she would have a great time reading about wolves.

Her mother wasn't there when Cassie got home from school. She checked the refrigerator—it was loaded with food. Good. Her mother had put away all the groceries and had gone shopping for clothes.

Cassie raced through her preparations for gardening, hauled the little red wagon out from under the porch, and walked quickly to the Ulmers'.

Mrs. Ulmer waved the newspaper at her. "The ad's in, and it looks good."

"My science teacher told me." She studied the lost and found column. It said just what she had wanted it to say. "How long before I get letters, do you s'pose?"

"A couple of days, I think. I told them I'd run the ad for at least a week. It might take even longer."

Cassie scuffed one foot on the sidewalk. "What if nobody answers?"

Mrs. Ulmer smiled. "Well, then, I think you'll really have a dog." She glanced at Cassie and looked puzzled. "That is what you want, isn't it?"

"Yeah, sure." Cassie swallowed hard. That would have been just great up until the day she realized that Tokie was a wolf. But what if no one answered the ad?

Mrs. Ulmer said, "Don't worry. Let's wait and see."

Cassie put the little red wagon away in the garage and went to work. She weeded a big stretch of the lawn and spaded half way around the roses. She finished by watering several more squares and then coiled up the hose.

Mrs. Ulmer came out and paid her. "I'm sorry we don't have a sprinkler system. I'll ask Mr. Ulmer to buy one of those big sprinklers that go in the middle of the lawn. You could turn it on before you go, and I could turn it off later."

"That would help a lot." She didn't want to be rude, but she didn't want to stand around talking. "I've got a lot to do at home. I'll be back tomorrow."

She hurried to the Catleton Arket, bought two large cans of dog food, each of a different variety, and hurried home. Her mother's car was still not in the driveway. What a relief, Cassie thought. She did her homework methodically and, when it was time, fixed Tokie's dinner. She had bought two different kinds of canned food so she could find out which he liked best. She opened the cans and emptied them in his dish, one flavor on each side, and put the fresh ground beef in the middle. She went outside and placed the dish beside the tree, remembering which flavor was on which side of the bowl.

Tokie appeared in a few minutes, approached her with his impish grin, and gave her face several wet kisses before going to his dish. He put one paw on the edge of the bowl, flipped it over, and gobbled up the ground beef. Cassie wished she had a dog dish he couldn't push over. He sniffed with interest at the canned food, gobbled up one kind, and then went after the other. Cassie smiled.

Tokie licked his muzzle and came to lean against her. He slobbered more kisses on her face and invited her for their walk. She had to hitch up her jeans again—she guessed the constant bending over for gardening had stretched them.

She made it all the way to the white rock without breathing hard. She sat and watched Tokie zigzag as usual up and down the hill. He suddenly crouched and froze. Cassie saw a rabbit some yards away, nibbling on a green plant. "Oh, no!" she said, remembering what had happened before, yet she couldn't look away. Tokie slowly crept closer and closer. And then, instead of pouncing on the rabbit, he sprang straight up in the air and landed stiff-legged on all fours where the rabbit had been. He went on leaping and bounding noisily around the hole where the animal had disappeared.

"Whew," said Cassie. "What kind of a hunter are you?"

She looked up to the top of the hill and remembered how she used to perch up there and survey the countryside. She smiled, stood up, and climbed the path all the way to the top.

Tokie frolicked about and chased butterflies, leaping up and snapping his jaws on empty air. Cassie thought she caught a gleam of mischief in his eyes. She laughed out loud. She guessed today was his day to tease rabbits and to be silly.

She found the old familiar shallow place in the rock where she could sit, and it was almost comfortable to lean back. She had forgotten how beautiful it was up here, how far she could see over the countryside. Down below her was a valley with big homes built along a winding street. A couple of the yards had swimming pools. She didn't remember seeing any houses there before. They must have been built since she had last hiked up here to the top. That was a couple of years ago.

Wow, she thought, pretty soon their house will

be surrounded by houses, and they won't be in the country anymore. Tokie wouldn't have been able to find his way to her house.

Cassie felt Tokie press himself against her leg, and with a start she came back to the present.

The sun dropped behind the hill. Cassie tried to coax Tokie to her to hug him. He frolicked once around the rock and swung across the hill out of sight. "Oh well," said Cassie, smiling. "Bye for now."

Cassie slid down from the boulders and followed the rabbit path to her yard.

Her mother was standing by the back door, a worried look on her face. "Where in the world have you been?" she asked.

CHAPTER
17

"I hiked up the hill to the big white rock," said Cassie. "Special science project."

"I wish you had left me a note," said her mother. "I always leave you a note to say where I'm going."

"I know," said Cassie. "I'm sorry I forgot."

Cassie went in the kitchen and took a deep breath. "Wow! Fried chicken! Great!"

Her mother said, "Anyway, supper's ready. I was afraid it would get cold."

"How was shopping for clothes?"

"Pretty good. There was a sale on at Guggenheimer's, and I got some really nice things. I'm glad I went."

Her mother's eyes were shining. It was good to see her happy, even if it was for the wrong reasons.

"I'd like to see them." The wolf book would wait.

"And you can tell me about your science project."

Cassie shrugged. "It's just about bushes and shrubs."

"You're not eating much. Are you feeling okay?" asked her mother. The fried chicken was good, but Cassie had eaten only three pieces. "After all, I fixed it because you love it."

"Mom, it's so good, I want to save some for after school."

After dinner her mother went in the bedroom to model the clothes. Cassie braced herself for seeing frilly party dresses, much too young looking for her mother.

Her mother came out in a slim purple dress with an oriental look. She looked terrific. It made Cassie feel funny. "That's great, Mom," she said. "I suppose that's for going out to dinner sometime?"

Her mother nodded. "It will look all right no matter what restaurant we go to."

Cassie noticed she said *we*. "What else did you get?"

The next was a dark print dress with a draped skirt and long sleeves. Her mother twirled and struck a pose like a real model. Cassie smiled. "Mom, that dress looks really good on you."

"That's not all. Wait till you see the last one. It's for a very special occasion."

Uh oh, Cassie thought. Here it comes.

Cassie wasn't expecting her mother to suddenly seem like a stranger. The straight, dark skirt reached almost to the floor, and the filmy ivory blouse had full sleeves and a lace collar that framed a face glowing with pleasure. Her mother looked great, Cassie admitted to herself. She didn't know whether to be glad or sorry.

"Wow!" she said at last. "You look really classy, Mom." She hesitated. "How are you going to pay for all that?"

Her mother struck another pose. "It looks like I'll be getting a raise. Ta dah!"

Cassie exclaimed, "Super! You deserve it, Mom!"

It must be a whopping big raise, thought Cassie, if that's what it really is. Funny that she didn't tell me before. "You've sure had a great day. Maybe you can celebrate by going to a movie tomorrow."

Her mother looked at her. "What's with this movie bit? You haven't said anything about one for months."

Cassie shrugged. "Just an idea. It's not important."

"Well, I want to sleep in tomorrow, and maybe I will go to the movies in the afternoon. I don't want to waste my day off! I'll phone some friends."

It looked as though Cassie wouldn't have to worry about her time with Toklata. She settled down with the book on wolves. She had always enjoyed stories and articles about them, but knowing a real wolf put everything in a different light. She turned the pages and realized how little she really knew about wolves. She had to change a lot of her ideas.

Wolves don't howl at the moon, they don't weigh two hundred pounds, they don't travel in packs of fifty, they're not bloodthirsty, and healthy wolves kill to eat, not for fun or sport like people do. She thought about Brad. She wondered what kind of a hunter he'd be if he had to eat everything he killed. She bet he'd stop shooting so many rabbits. Even healthy wolves don't kill every animal they can.

Cassie hadn't known that a pack of wolves is really

an extended family of wolves—the alpha or lead pair, several generations of their pups, and occasionally a litter from another pair.

She read on, fascinated.

Some wolves specialize in killing small game, like mice or rabbits, and some wolves never hunt or kill at all. The wolves who are hunters provide food for the wolf pups. Wolves take better care of each other in a pack than a lot of humans do of their own families, Cassie thought.

Then she read how friendly the wolves are toward each other, playing tag together, romping with the pups, and teaching the pups things they should know. She wondered if Tokie had other wolves to play with where he lived. Probably, she thought. He must be really lonely. Maybe that's why he was so happy to have her as a friend. Maybe looking for his owner was a better idea than she thought.

She read, "A wolf cannot ever be 'tamed,' but he can be socialized." Cassie wondered, what does *that* mean? Mr. Crowell would know.

The next day during study hall, she looked through the regular school library. There wasn't anything on wolves, but there was another book on Alaska. She checked that out. When the bell rang for science period, she went to Mr. Crowell's desk.

"That wolf book you loaned me is awfully interesting. I'm halfway through already. What does it mean when it says that wolves cannot be tamed, but they can be socialized?"

Mr. Crowell rocked back and forth. "It means that wolves can be brought up to get along with other animals, even with humans, but they cannot ever be trained or domesticated like dogs and cats."

"Oh. I'd really like to read more about wolves. Could you get me some other books on wolves from the public library? It's too far away for me to get to."

Mr. Crowell smiled. "I'll see what I can do."

"I wish we could do a unit on wolves in our class."

He frowned, rocked some more, then nodded thoughtfully. "All our units are planned for this term, but I can work it into the next semester."

Cassie opened the book on Alaska. When Joe glanced at it, he saw the photos of sled dogs. He leaned over and asked in a half-whisper, "You got your Eskimo dog yet?"

Cassie shook her head. "I'm not going to get an Eskimo dog after all. I decided that's not the right kind of dog for southern California."

"Yeah, you're prob'ly right. Too bad. Last night on TV, I saw some sled dogs pulling kids on skate boards. I thought maybe your Eskimo dog could do something like that." He grinned.

"How big is your dog, Skunk?"

Joe looked surprised. "Pretty big. You think maybe Skunk could pull a skate board?"

"If he's big and strong, sure. You said he's a mixed breed, and they're usually pretty smart. I'll bet he could learn. I just read a book on training dogs. It wouldn't be hard."

"Maybe you can show me how to teach him. After school, when cross-country season is over?"

Cassie was confused. "I guess so. Sure. I'll show you how to train your dog."

Joe rolled his eyes. "I can see Skunk and me spinning down Main Street."

In a huddle Brad was talking to some of the boys about hunting, and Cassie couldn't help overhearing.

"Out in the desert, I got four out of five rabbits on the run. Now that is really cool."

Then he said something that made Cassie's blood freeze.

"There must be a lot of rabbits on the hills behind Larkspur Lane. I think I'll go up there after school sometime and peg a few."

Cassie lived on Larkspur Lane, and those were the hills where she and Tokie went hiking, where Toklata probably lived. What if Brad saw Tokie up there? Brad was just the kind of kid who might think shooting a dog running fast would be fun. She needed desperately to find Tokie's owner. The rest of the day went by as though she were in a dream, a nightmare.

When Cassie got home, she found a note on the kitchen table from her mother. "Am going out to dinner with Fred. Home later."

Cassie moaned. Tokie's life was in danger of Brad's hunting, and her mom was going out to dinner twice within one week with the same guy. That was serious. Cassie's life was one problem after another.

She got up and headed for her candy bars.

C H A P T E R
18

On her way to the candy bars, Cassie looked at her watch. She was late! Mrs. Ulmer liked people to be prompt. Cassie grabbed one candy bar, hurried into her gardening clothes, and practically ran down the walk.

Mrs. Ulmer was glad to see her. "I got some chrysanthemum plants. Where shall we put them?"

They decided on a corner of the yard by the sidewalk. There were six little plants with some yellow blooms beginning to show. They brightened the whole yard. At the end of an hour, Cassie uncoiled the hose and watered the yard where she planned to work next.

Mrs. Ulmer watched her and said, "I ought to ask Mr. Ulmer to buy one of those big sprinklers you can put in the middle of the lawn. You could turn it on before you go, and I could turn it off later."

Cassie chewed on her lower lip, hesitating. "That's what you said the other day."

Mrs. Ulmer frowned. "I did?"

"I'm pretty sure. I thought it was a good idea."

"Oh," said Mrs. Ulmer. "I'm sorry. I'll try to remember." She shook her head. "I must be getting old. I can remember every one of Danny's words when he was starting to talk, but I can't remember what I did the day before yesterday. I used to help Mr. Ulmer in the store, keeping track of his orders and taking inventory, but I couldn't begin to do that now." She sighed heavily. "He sometimes teases me about forgetting, but he says he's really having a hard time without my help." She suddenly smiled at Cassie. "Tell me, how's your white dog?"

Cassie turned off the hose, wiped her hands on her jeans, and sat down on the steps. "He's okay. When do you think I might hear something from the ad?"

"Soon, probably. Why don't you walk your dog over here to see me someday, before your ad gets answered?"

Cassie hesitated. "He doesn't have a leash. I haven't put a collar on him yet."

"Not very well trained, is he?"

Cassie changed the subject. "I think I'll ask Mom to get some chrysanthemums for our yard, too. They sure look nice."

On her way home she saw the animal control truck again.

The lady officer was at the wheel. Cassie waved to her, and the truck pulled to the curb and stopped.

"How's the search going?" asked Cassie.

The officer shook her head. "Two more sightings, and one of them said they thought it looked like a *wolf.* They didn't get a good look though. It's definitely in this neighborhood, and I wouldn't want anyone to shoot him. Would you watch for him and let me know?"

"Sure I will," Cassie said, and then, "If someone tries to shoot him, what would you do?"

"Wolves are a protected species. If it turns out to be a wolf, Fish and Game would probably put the hunter in jail. If he had a hunting license, he'd pay a big fine and certainly lose his license. Unfortunately, if the police see a wolf, they'll probably just shoot it to protect the public."

"There's a boy in my class who has his hunting license and goes hunting a lot with his dad. He brags about being able to shoot rabbits on the run. Yesterday he said he was going to come up here in these hills to hunt rabbits. I'm worried that he might shoot that white dog while it was running just to see if he could."

"First of all, it's against the law to discharge firearms in a residential area. You might tell him that."

"I can try," Cassie said slowly. "Suppose the animal *is* a wolf, or part wolf, how will you catch him?"

"We certainly wouldn't try to catch him like we would a dog. That's a completely different problem. A wolf could bite right through the noose that we use. I've been checking around. We would have to trap him inside a fence. I noticed that there's a house with a swimming pool a half-mile or so from here, and the pool has a pretty high iron fence all around it. We'll put some fresh meat out by the pool for bait and fix it so the gate closes as soon as the animal goes in."

"Then what would you do?"

"We'd tranquilize him with a special gun, and after he was asleep, we'd put him in the truck."

"And then what?" asked Cassie.

The officer looked at her. "Do you know something that I don't know? About this dog?"

Cassie said, "Well, I think I saw him up on the hill. He *is* beautiful."

"Next time you see him, please give me a call right away, even if it's after hours. My name's Sally." She handed Cassie her business card with her home phone number written in at the bottom.

Why did the officer want her to call her at home after hours? Cassie wondered. Something wasn't right. She looked at the officer. "You said before, you thought he'd be adopted pretty quickly from the pound. Is that true?"

Sally sat still. "Well, I honestly don't want to take him to the pound. If he's part wolf, they won't consider him adoptable, and they will have to put him to sleep."

Cassie drew in her breath sharply.

"Unfortunately, part wolves are commercially valuable. The demand for animals like that is growing fast. People think they make good guard dogs and will pay a lot for one, even a young pup. But they do not make good pets, so that's why the pound can't let them be adopted."

"What if he really *is* a wolf?"

"He still couldn't go to the pound. They used to relocate wild animals, like bears and so on, up in the mountains where they would turn them loose, but that's too expensive now. Fish and Game has shooters, professional marksmen, and they'd shoot the wolf."

"Wouldn't a real wolf belong to somebody?"

There was a long silence. "A friend of mine out in San Fernando Valley trains animals for the movies. I really would like to take the animal to him."

Cassie shook her head. "I'm not sure that's a good idea. I read somewhere that a wolf can't be trained, he can only be socialized."

"I'll ask my friend about it first," Sally said. "I'm sure he'll know. He has all kinds of animals at his place." She waved and drove off.

At home, Cassie postponed her homework and poured over the book about wolves that Mr. Crowell had loaned her. She was surprised to read that even though each wolf within a pack has his own personality and character, the wolves can work together, even though they are so different.

Cassie thought about that as she fixed Tokie's dinner and went outside. Tokie again was waiting for her and frolicked to meet her. She put down his dish and braced herself for his joyful welcome. She knelt down to have him practically wash her whole face with his tongue before he went after his dinner. She waited on the steps while he ate and promptly got to her feet when he invited her for a walk. She hitched up her jeans again and hiked all the way to the top of the hill. She sat and watched Tokie zigzag as usual up and down the hill.

She settled herself on top of the boulder, closed her eyes, and imagined that she was a member of a wolf pack, all kinds of wolves getting along together.

After a while she felt Tokie paw at her legs, and she opened her eyes. With a start she came back to the present.

Tokie grinned at her, swung his tail twice, and trotted off around the hill. Cassie slid down from the boulders and followed the rabbit path to her yard, wondering what her mother would say about the dinner date. She fixed herself some supper, finished her homework, and climbed into bed with the wolf book propped up on her knees.

Cassie turned the page and almost laughed out loud. Wolves like to scare each other by pouncing on sleeping wolves or by jumping out in front of one another from hiding places! She didn't dream that wolves had a sense of humor, but she had seen it for herself. Tokie could be a real clown.

She was still smiling when she heard her mother's car on the driveway.

"You're still up," said her mother, pausing in the doorway to Cassie's room.

"I've been reading." Cassie wanted to be casual about her mother's date. "Oh, I forgot to tell you. Miss Kimura, you know, the Japanese lady who lives three doors down, wants me to rake her lawn because the gardener's leaf-blower machine is too noisy. She'll pay me. I said I could on Saturdays. Is that okay?"

Her mother frowned. "I guess it's all right. I wish

you wouldn't get friendly with her. I used to work the night shift, and when I came home late, there were always lights on in her house and cars on her driveway and men going in and out."

"Oh," said Cassie. She remembered Miss Kimura not saying anything about her work. "Okay, Mom." But she could rake the lawn without being friendly. "How was your dinner date?"

C H A P T E R
19

Her mom smiled. "It was a super evening. We went to a place called The Outrigger. It's way up on a hill-side and a stream runs in front of it, so you have to walk over a bridge to get in."

It sounded romantic, Cassie thought. "What about the food?"

"Just great. It was a luau, and I ate too much."

"Are you going to see him again?"

There was a long pause. Her mother looked embarrassed.

"Well, he wants to take me to a special restaurant in Ventura next Thursday."

"Ventura!" Cassie felt hot and cold at the same time. "Mom, that's over on the coast! That is *hours* from here!"

"I know. Tomorrow I'm going to ask the manager if he'll let me have Thursday afternoon off." She smiled at Cassie. "Good night and sweet dreams," she said and went off down the hall, humming softly.

Sweet dreams, baloney, thought Cassie in despair. This affair was going much too fast. Her mother wouldn't get back until the early hours of the morning. Ventura! Why couldn't they just find another restaurant someplace near?

She closed the book on wolves and lay staring up at the ceiling. She had already decided she might use her mother's boyfriend, Fred, to keep her mother out of Tokie's way and then get rid of Fred later. Maybe this was the time. Her mother would be gone all Thursday afternoon and evening with Fred—Cassie needed to use that free time for something special.

She would coax Toklata into the house! She wanted him to be comfortable in her house in case she had to hide him from animal control and from Brad, if he went hunting in the hills behind her house. Her mother would never know about it.

After class a group of the students gathered around Brad. Cassie stood still, staring at him, wishing she had the courage to speak up and tell another side of hunting, her side.

"He's such a dork," said a familiar voice behind her. "Doesn't it make you mad when he talks about hunting like he does?" Cassie turned and saw Lindsay glaring at Brad.

"Yeah," said Cassie, surprised.

"I can't stand people who hunt for sport or whatever you call it," Lindsay said. A hope in Cassie's heart flared up. Lindsay wanted to be friends again. "Come on, Lindsay," Joanna tugged at Lindsay's arm. "We're going for ice-cream cones. Forget about this 'save the animals' stuff."

Lindsay gestured as though to say to Cassie, "What

can I do?" She turned and walked away with Shannon and Joanna. Cassie's hope flickered and died.

Cassie wanted to tell Brad it was illegal to hunt in the residential part of town, but today wasn't a good day for that. There were too many kids gathered around him, admiring him. Maybe she would tell him tomorrow before class started.

But he wasn't in class the next day.

"Brad is home sick," said Mr. Crowell. Two of the boys in class snickered. Then it was Cassie who felt sick, thinking of Brad not sick at all but maybe in the hills where Toklata was hanging out. She could hardly wait to get home after school. She definitely had to get Tokie into the house. She made a plan.

After gardening that afternoon, she bought extra dog food. She went home from the Catleton Arket with four cans of dog food thumping against her shoulders in the backpack.

Miss Kimura was sitting on the front porch drinking what looked like iced tea. "Hello there," she said, smiling. "I'll see you on Saturday for the leaves, won't I?"

"Sure thing," said Cassie. "What kind of work did you say you do?"

Miss Kimura laughed. "I'm a computer software engineer, and that's why I have to have quiet for working. No noisy leaf blowers!"

"Computers!" exclaimed Cassie with a stab of envy. "I wish I knew more about computers."

"Come on in the house, and I'll show you what I do."

Cassie hesitated. Computers were okay, she

decided, and turned and walked up to the porch. Miss Kimura stood up and opened the front door. She led the way into the living room.

A radio was playing classical music softly. Cassie looked around at everything. The furniture was very oriental, and there were beautiful Japanese prints of landscapes on the walls. Just off the living room was a darkened room with a lot of books and a computer, the screen glowing a pale blue in the dark. Cassie was fascinated.

"I found out your name is Cassandra. Why don't you call me Karen?"

"Okay. Then you can call me Cassie."

Karen went into the darkened room and flicked on the light. "Here's where I do most of my work. I work during the day at Microtek Company in Los Angeles, but I'm getting ready to start my own company. A couple of the people I work with are going in with me on it. We work on it at night."

"Mom said she saw your lights on at night sometimes."

"I'm not surprised. We're designing a computer program for small businesses, like programs doctors and dentists already have for their offices. Ours would be for drug stores and gift shops and health-food stores, to keep track of orders and inventory."

"Grocery stores, maybe?"

"Small independent ones, of course. The big chains already do."

Cassie grinned. "I know somebody who could use that."

"Good. I'd like you to tell me about it when we've got our product ready."

"I will. I'd sure like to know more about computers."

"Maybe some evening when you're home and I need a break, you could come over and I'll show you how to use my computer."

"Oh boy," said Cassie. "I'd sure love that. Our math class has four computers, but there are thirty kids in the class so I hardly ever get a turn."

Karen looked interested. "What's the name of your school?"

"John C. Fremont Junior High. Our teacher tried to get another computer, but the school doesn't have enough money."

"That's too bad. Anyway, it will be fun teaching you."

Cassie went home smiling.

She awoke the next morning even before her alarm went off, and a shiver of excitement ran through her. Today was the day she was going to invite Toklata into the house. She had to familiarize him with the house in case he should ever be in danger. She hurried through breakfast, put her school work in the backpack, and started out the door. Shannon and Joanna were on the sidewalk nearing her house. Cassie hesitated. How she wished they were her friends, and Lindsay, too. She longed to talk with them. Then she remembered their sly looks and giggles. She stepped back inside, closed the door, and leaned against it. Several minutes later, she started for school.

When she walked into her homeroom, Lindsay and Shannon and Joanna were talking in low voices with their heads together. They stopped talking when Cassie entered.

Lindsay smiled and nodded to her. "Oh, hi, Cassie," she said, as though they were casual acquaintances.

"Hi," said Cassie. She longed for the days of friendship, the comfort of knowing that someone else felt almost exactly as she did. She plodded from one class to another the rest of the day.

Mr. Crowell had two more books on wolves for her, and she thanked him gratefully. After school Mrs. Ulmer was waiting for her on the front porch, waving some envelopes.

"Here are three answers to your ad," she called out, and Cassie hurried to take them.

"What do they say?"

"I didn't open them. Mr. Ulmer picked them up at the newspaper office this morning." She sat down on the chair on the front porch and motioned to Cassie to sit on the steps. "Here's a letter opener."

Cassie read aloud the first letter. "That white dog is mine. I lost my dog in October. Give me your address and I'll come to pick him up." There was a phone number.

"Humph," said Mrs. Ulmer. "He doesn't describe the dog. He didn't say anything more than what you put in the ad. Can't be the real owner."

Cassie sighed with relief. "The next one says, 'I lost my big white dog a couple months ago and maybe he's the dog you found. He's mostly white but has black tips on his ears and dark fur around his eyes. He answers to the name of Robbie.'" Cassie shook her head. "Too bad it's not his. Tokie is pure white."

She opened the third letter. The childish handwriting wasn't easy to read. "My dog was hit by a car last month and I miss him a lot. If you'll let me have the white dog I will give him a good home and lots of food and love." The letter saddened Cassie. "None of them is Tokie's real owner."

"I'm sure there will be more letters tomorrow."

When her gardening was finished, she hurried home, raced through her homework, and filled Toklata's dish with the dog food. She propped the back door open with an old pair of her father's work shoes and put Tokie's dish just inside the doorway. She put some ground beef inside the refrigerator, toward the front where she could get it quickly. She sat down at the kitchen table with a view of the back steps and waited.

When Tokie appeared in the shadows, he sniffed at the empty spot where he usually found his dish. He looked puzzled, paced quickly around the yard, and pointed his muzzle in the air, sniffing. Cautiously he approached the back steps.

Cassie spoke from inside the house. "Your dinner's in the back hall. Come on up, Tokie."

C H A P T E R
20

Tokie's tail swung slowly. He put one paw on the bottom step, hesitated, and looked all around. He took another step and repeated the process until he had carefully mounted the stairs. When at last he was on the porch, he only glanced at his dish and then stared in fascination through the back door into the hallway. Cassie smothered a giggle.

One foot at a time, he got as far as the doorway. There he leaned forward and stretched himself out as far as possible without moving his feet. He stood on tiptoe to peer into the hall, caught sight of Cassie at the kitchen table, and wrinkled his lips in his impish grin.

Cassie's heart pounded, but she sat still. "Good boy," she said. "Come on in."

Toklata leaned forward again and sniffed in the direction of the work shoes. He took a cautious step into the back hall and put his nose into one of the shoes, sniffing deeply.

"No, no!" said Cassie. "Leave those shoes alone."

Tokie looked up at her and swung his tail. He sniffed again toward the kitchen. Slowly he advanced into the kitchen, two careful steps forward and one step back, while Cassie held her breath. He came to her at last and leaned hard against her legs, twisting his head to peer up at her.

His golden eyes had a strange, penetrating look, and Cassie felt her heart skip a beat. Tokie seemed to be suddenly reassured. He began pacing slowly around the kitchen, peering from time to time into the living room. He paced more and more quickly until he was darting back and forth between the back door and the door to the living room. Cassie, smiling, got up and walked into the living room, talking to Toklata as she went. She sat down in the arm chair and waited.

He went through the same ritual of stepping one cautious paw at a time into the living room and slowly worked his way to where Cassie sat in the arm chair. He sniffed the chair deeply, then went to the sofa and sniffed long and hard each of the sofa cushions and the little throw pillows. Without warning he jumped up on the sofa, growled ferociously, and attacked one of the little pillows.

Cassie jumped up. "Oh no! Don't do that!" she exclaimed, hurrying to the sofa. It was the oldest pillow but her mother's favorite.

Tokie ignored her. He put one paw on the pillow and pulled with his teeth. The sound of ripping cloth sent him into a frenzy. He shook the pillow, and feathers filled the air. Toklata crouched over his new possession, his tail waving hard. Through the cloud of feathers, Cassie reached a hand to rescue the pillow. Toklata's white fangs shone, and he snarled.

Cassie, shocked, snatched back her hand. "Please don't," she begged, retreating a few steps. Tokie wildly shook the last shreds of the pillow. Feathers filled the entire room and settled on the rug and furniture. He jumped down onto the floor, tossed the remains of the pillow over his shoulder, and waved his tail happily at Cassie, grinning his lopsided grin. She shuddered.

Before she knew it, Tokie had leaped back onto the sofa, sniffed deeply at the middle cushion, and had begun digging hard and fast into the cushion with his front paws. His long sharp toenails ripped the cloth, and foam stuffing flew in clumps across the room.

Cassie panicked. Hurriedly she backed into the kitchen, opened the refrigerator, and pulled out the plate of ground beef. She waved it in front of her and called to Toklata. He looked up from the sofa, hesitated, sniffed, and dashed into the kitchen, shedding feathers and foam stuffing as he came. Cassie quickly put down the plate. "There," she said.

The wolf put one paw on the plate and flipped the meat onto the floor. He chased it around with his nose and finally gulped it down. Then he turned his head sideways, opened his huge jaws, and closed his back teeth on the plate. It snapped into several pieces.

"Don't!" shrieked Cassie. Tokie crunched happily on the pottery while Cassie stood aghast. Pieces of the plate lay in slobbers on the floor and then disappeared down his throat.

"Quit it," implored Cassie. Maybe he thought he was eating bones. Thinking fast, she edged past him as he munched away and went onto the porch. "Here's your dinner," she said, pushing the bowl with one foot.

Tokie ignored her. He went back into the living room, and she could hear him attacking the sofa again. How could she get him out of the living room and away from the sofa?

She hurried into her bedroom and spied the rubber mouse she had bought at the Catleton Arket. Holding it out in front of her, she squeaked it rapidly. Tokie soon appeared in the hall, his head cocked. Some feathers still clung to his ears. She bounced the toy on the floor to him.

He knew right away she was just trying to distract him. He sniffed the toy mouse, pushed it aside with his nose, and looked up at her to grin. Again he cocked his head to one side and swung his tail slowly.

"What am I going to do with you?" exclaimed Cassie. This was a disaster!

Tokie looked with interest around her room, advanced slowly in to the center, and began sniffing thoroughly everything in turn—the bed, the chair at her desk, the dresser. The closet door was open, and he planted his front feet and leaned forward to peer inside. One step, then another. . . . He found the pile of dirty clothes on the closet floor and shoved his nose into it, taking deep breaths. He backed out with one of her socks dangling from his mouth. He threw the sock up in the air and caught it several times.

He threw it into a corner. He crouched and crept up on it, finally pouncing on it from ambush. He killed it three or four times, tossing it in the air and attacking it again and again.

Finally Tokie trotted around the bedroom with the mangled sock in his mouth as though to say, "See what I've got." He kept eyeing her bed, and suddenly he jumped up on it and raked away at the covers with his front feet. When he had the covers in a turmoil, he turned around several times and lay down, holding the sock between his paws. He cuddled it and began alternately to lick it and nibble on it.

"Whew!" said Cassie. She collapsed onto the chair. How was she going to get him outside?

She picked up the squeaky mouse, cradled it in her arms so Tokie couldn't see it, and began talking softly to it as though it were alive. Shutting her eyes to the chaos in the living room, she walked through the kitchen, laughing and talking to the mouse and making it squeak as though it were carrying on a conversation with her and returning her laughter.

With loud steps she marched into the back hall and out the back door. On her way she carried the dish of dog food to the tree and left it. She sat down on the bottom step and continued her laughing and talking with the rubber mouse.

Out of the corner of her eye, she watched the back door. After a while Tokie appeared in the back hall, sniffing and checking out everything that interested him. He dropped the sock and picked up one of her father's shoes. The door began to swing shut, and

Tokie hesitated. Cassie jumped up and jogged around the back yard, waving and squeaking the rubber mouse. Tokie hung onto the shoe and dashed down the steps to join Cassie. The back door clicked shut.

Whew! Cassie watched with relief as Tokie raced around the backyard, the shoe dangling from his mouth. She laughed and waved the rubber mouse under his nose, then hid it behind her. Tokie cocked his head to one side, swung his tail, dropped the shoe, and made a dive for the mouse. She let go of it and hurried up the steps into the house. Firmly she shut the door behind her. She would worry about the shoe later.

Thank heavens her mother had gone to Ventura and wouldn't be home till after midnight. It took hours to vacuum up the feathers, but she finally got them all. Or as many as she could see. She put away the vacuum and buried the shredded remains of the pillow in the trash can. She would worry later about what to tell her mother. She stuck the foam stuffing back into the sofa cushion as best she could, turned the cushion upside down, and put it back on the sofa so the rip wouldn't show.

She looked at the kitchen clock and gasped. Eleven o'clock at night, and she had not even thought about supper! No wonder she was exhausted. She made herself a peanut butter and jelly sandwich and sat down at the table, wondering what to do next with her wolf.

She had learned one thing. She would never again invite Tokie inside. She loved him, but he was a disaster in the house. He was not a pet, he was a wolf. She would have to think of another way to keep him safe.

She fixed her bed where Tokie had almost wrecked it and crawled under the covers. She closed her eyes, and the next thing she knew her alarm was ringing and sunlight was forming a square on her bedroom carpet.

It lit up a single white feather, and Cassie groaned.

CHAPTER
21

Cassie put the feather in her wastebasket and hurried to get dressed. She had to check out the house in daylight, before her mother had a chance to look at it. Her mother's bedroom door was shut, so she knew her mother had gotten home from Ventura.

Cassie had missed only a few feathers last night. The sofa cushion that Tokie had started to dig into and Cassie had turned over looked cleaner than the others. She turned over the other two cushions to match. She surveyed the room carefully. It looked okay. She swept the kitchen floor and washed the place where Tokie had messed the meat around before he ate it—and the plate. If she had missed anything, she hoped her mother would miss it too. She hurried off to school.

She looked for Brad with anticipation in science class, but he was still absent. Maybe he really *was* sick. She hoped so.

She hoped and prayed there would be more letters at the Ulmers' answering her ad. She hurried home to change into her clothes for gardening. Just as she was leaving the house to go to the Ulmers', she heard two gunshots up in the hills behind her house.

Cassie's heart almost stopped. She didn't dare call the police because of Tokie. Should she hike up to find Brad or whoever was shooting and tell them that shooting was illegal in a residential area?

Several more shots split the silence. She made up her mind. She would phone Mrs. Ulmer to say she wasn't feeling well—which was certainly true—and go up the hill to find out who was shooting and at what.

Mrs. Ulmer was very sympathetic. "That's too bad. I hope you're not coming down with something. We'll see how you feel tomorrow."

"Oh, I wanted to tell you. My neighbor, Miss Kimura, asked me to start working for her on Saturdays. She wants me to rake her lawn by hand because she hates the leaf blower her gardener uses."

Mrs. Ulmer laughed. "I don't blame her. I never wanted a gardener because all they did was mow, blow, and go. If you're feeling well enough, why don't you go to her house tomorrow instead of coming here? Our yard is looking much better now."

"That would be great," said Cassie. She hung up the phone and looked out the front window to see if the animal control truck was anywhere in sight. It wasn't.

Where are you, Sally, when I need you? Cassie hiked up the hill to the white rock, peering around and listening as she went. She climbed all the way to the top. There was no more shooting. She stood on the highest boulder and looked all over the country.

She didn't see anyone at all. She finally went home, hoping the hunter had gone home, too.

She surveyed the inside of their house again and decided she had been lucky to get it in order before her mother saw it. She wished there had been some way to keep Tokie from attacking the little pillow and the sofa cushion. She'd have to teach Tokie what was hers and what was his. She was sure he hadn't snarled at her intending to attack. She stretched out on her bed with the wolf book. She could read until it was time to fix Tokie's dinner.

She turned the pages slowly, trying to find a chapter about training a wolf. She found it, but to her dismay, it wasn't what she wanted at all. She read that a wolf cannot be trained like a dog or a horse because it won't submit to any rules except the ones made by its own wolf society and wolf pack. A wolf will not learn people rules.

That was a shock. But it explained why Tokie had snarled at her when she reached for the pillow. *He* had the pillow first, so it belonged to *him*. He was a wild creature, a wolf. She would have to love him just as he was. And I do, she sighed.

She thought about yesterday's destruction. Now she was certain that Tokie would be happier and better off in his own home, wherever it was. But what if his owner never saw her ad? Was there any other way to find the owner?

She remembered Mr. Crowell had told her class about the SPCA, which takes care of stray animals.

In the phone book, the Society for Prevention of Cruelty to Animals was listed in big black letters. She dialed their number, and a woman answered.

Cassie cleared her throat. It would probably be best not to give her own name. "This is . . . Jenny Adams," she said and asked if she could talk to someone who owned a wolf. The woman said if anyone wanted to talk to the owner of a wolf, they would have to know the owner's name.

"But how do I find out when I don't know his name?"

There was a long pause. The woman said carefully, "If you have found an animal, whether it's a dog or a coyote or whatever, give us your address, and we'll come and pick it up. We will do everything we can to find the owner. The animal will be much safer in the shelter here than wandering the streets where it might get hit by a car."

"Okay, thanks," said Cassie, and she hung up quickly. She was glad she hadn't given her real name. She thought again about calling Sally, the animal control officer. Cassie still had her card. But if Sally found Toklata, he wouldn't be returned to his owner. He would go to the animal trainer in San Fernando Valley.

Mr. Crowell was her last hope for saving Tokie. She had his phone number; she could tell him the whole story and see if he could keep Brad from hunting in the hills. She wasn't sure what he could do to help Tokie. She only knew he would think of something.

Her mind was in turmoil by the time she went outside to put Tokie's dinner under the tree. She sat down on the steps and waited for him.

He didn't appear. After a while she was uneasy, and then she was scared. She waited and waited, and still he didn't come.

Her mother would be home soon. She left Tokie's dinner by the tree and went into the house, feeling miserable. What if Tokie had been shot? She stretched out on her bed with the wolf book, but she couldn't concentrate on the words.

The front door opened and shut.

"Hi, I'm home." Her mother's voice was cheerful.

"Did you have a good time in Ventura yesterday?" asked Cassie in a casual voice as she went in to the living room.

"We surely did. Last night we had dinner in this really great restaurant! It's like a farmhouse, real homey, with a country atmosphere. The food was super. It's the kind of restaurant I wish I worked in. It's called The Spinning Wheel. Isn't that a nice name?"

"Was it worth driving all that way?"

"Oh my yes." Her mother smiled as though it were more than worth it. "What are you going to fix for supper?"

Was she trying to change the subject? Cassie said, "The leftover fried chicken. It sure is good." But she wasn't hungry at all.

Several times during supper, Cassie tried to find out more about her mother's trip to Ventura, but her mother wouldn't talk about it. Maybe she feels guilty going out with a man while she's still married to my father, thought Cassie. At least her mother was still wearing her wedding ring.

Her mother asked her if she was feeling okay, and Cassie said, "Not really." She picked at her food.

"Maybe you'd better sleep in tomorrow."

"I'll see how I feel."

Before she went to bed, she looked at Tokie's dish under the tree. The food was still there—untouched.

She would look for him tomorrow if he hadn't come for his dinner by then. She tried to read, turning the pages carefully. There was a section on the family life of wolves. A pair usually mated for life. Just then, Cassie figured out how to get rid of Fred What's-his-name when she needed to. When Cassie finally met him, she could say, "Oh, my father phoned today. He's coming home this evening. I'm sure you'll want to meet him." She practiced saying the lines, wondering how soon the man would disappear.

She couldn't sleep at all. She tossed and turned in bed, her heart banging inside her chest as she thought of her wolf maybe lying dead or wounded up in the hills somewhere. If Tokie was still alive, she had to get him inside her house one more time. That way, no one could shoot him before she had a chance to find his owner. She'd figure out a way to pen him in a room somewhere. A wolf in the house would be a disaster, but that would be better than having him killed.

CHAPTER
22

Saturday morning Cassie dressed quickly and went outside to look at Tokie's dish. All the food was still there. Her heart sank.

There are lots of reasons why Tokie didn't show up, she told herself. She shouldn't jump to conclusions. She'd work at Karen's, and when she had finished, she'd go up the hill again to look for her wolf.

She didn't feel like eating anything. After a while she walked three doors down to Karen's house. Karen answered the doorbell. She was wearing jeans and a tee shirt that read, "I program in C because it's the only language I can spell." She stood in the doorway, smiling, as Cassie read the words.

"What does that mean?" asked Cassie.

"In computers there are different 'languages' you can use for programming. They have names like Pascal and Fortran and so on. There's one called C, just like it's spelled."

"Oh," said Cassie. "That's funny."

"I thought so. I'm glad you could come. There are two rakes in the garage, so pick the one you want. Here are some trash bags for the leaves. When you've finished, come on in. I made some lemonade for us, and I have a surprise for you."

Cassie wondered what the surprise was. She chose a rake from the garage and worked quickly. The lawn was thick with dead leaves from the sycamores. She filled six trash bags, jamming the leaves in, and then rang the doorbell.

The door opened and Cassie said, "I've finished."

Karen looked out at the lawn. "Already? You're a fast worker. It certainly looks better. Come have some lemonade."

On the wood-block table in the kitchen were two tall glasses with ice in them. Karen put a big pitcher of lemonade beside them and filled the glasses.

"Your mother's gone to work, hasn't she? If you'd like to, you could spend the day here with me in case you're worried about being safe, and I'll tell you about the surprise.

Cassie, puzzled, asked, "What do you mean, worried about being safe?"

Karen's smile faded. "I guess you haven't heard. I don't have time to watch TV, so I listen to the radio. I work better with classical music playing. But they just had a news flash on the radio about a wolf."

"Wolf!" choked Cassie. "What wolf?"

"It was just on the news that a wolf has been sighted, right here in our neighborhood!"

Cassie gasped. "A wolf! Oh my gosh!"

"Well, they think it's a wolf. I didn't know there could be a wolf in a neighborhood like this. I bought this house because it was so quiet here."

"A wolf! When did they see him?"

Karen said, "Just this morning."

"This morning!" exclaimed Cassie. Then Tokie wasn't dead! She felt like laughing and crying from relief and joy, but she pretended to be shocked. "Oh my gosh!"

"I don't think we have to worry. They're sending out the sheriff and his posse to take care of him. You'll be safe here with me until they've caught him. I sure would hate to see someone get hurt."

"OH MY GOODNESS!" exclaimed Cassie. Now she really *was* shocked. She leaped to her feet. "I just remembered something *really important.* I've got to go home right away." She headed for the door.

"You haven't drunk your lemonade!" Karen exclaimed. "And I wanted to tell you about the surprise I have for you."

"I'll be back later!"

"You be careful. I'll tell you when you get back."

"Okay," said Cassie, and she bolted for home. Just as she ran down the walk, the County Animal Control truck went by in a big hurry. Cassie ran out into the street and yelled and jumped up and down, waving her arms. The truck slowed, stopped, and backed up.

Sally leaned out of the window. "Hop in!" she said. "I'm on my way to the house with the swimming pool. That white dog may be a wolf after all, and I'm going to put out some ground beef for bait to catch him."

Cassie said, "No thanks. I have to go home."

"What did you want to see me about?" asked the officer.

159

Cassie gulped. "A neighbor just told me about the wolf. I wanted to ask you if that was really true."

"I guess so, though I haven't seen him yet. Sure you don't want to come along? You've been interested in him."

"I wish I could, but I can't," Cassie said. "There's something awfully important I have to do. Thanks anyway."

Sally shrugged. "Suit yourself." She drove off.

There seemed to be a lot of cars around, more than usual, coming and going and parking along the curb. There was even a white van with a TV camera mounted on the roof. On the side was printed "Channel 29 ABC News Team." Cassie was alarmed. She hurried through the house, opened the back door, and stood outside, listening. She propped the door open and trembled.

Far away she heard men's voices shouting at each other. She heard one deep voice bellowing on a bullhorn.

Three gunshots echoed through the hills. Then a fourth. Cassie's mouth went dry. She saw something white up on the hill. It was Tokie, slinking from one bush to another, looking occasionally over his shoulder in a puzzled fashion.

Cassie was horrified. He doesn't know they're shooting at him, she thought. He's probably never even heard gun shots. . . . He's been brought up with people. They'll shoot him, and he'll never have a chance.

She walked into the middle of the yard and clapped

160

her hands to attract Tokie's attention. She thought, I must get him down here, but I mustn't let him know I'm scared. At the sound of the clapping, Tokie came out of the bushes and looked down the hill toward her. She cupped her hands and called softly, "Tokie, here! *Tokie, here!*"

Another gunshot. The wolf faltered in his tracks for a fraction of a second, then melted into the bushes.

Cassie ran across the yard and partway up the hill. Tokie appeared in a clearing, swinging his tail.

"Good Tokie, good boy," said Cassie, thinking fast of the things she had learned about wolves. She dropped to her knees and held out her arms. "Good Tokie."

The wolf moved hesitantly down the hill toward her and ended with a little rush into her arms, washing her face with his long tongue. She hugged him and then dug her fingers into the long thick fur around his neck. If only he wore a collar, she thought. His ruff would have to do. She stood up, holding firmly onto the thick ruff of fur. "Let's go home, Tokie," she said, tugging as though she had him on a leash, and she took a step toward the house. Step-by-step she got him across the yard to the foot of the stairs.

There he planted his front legs and wouldn't move.

He was looking up the hill, and his fur rose along his back. Cassie looked up the hill and saw something moving from one bush to another. It was a man, dressed in camouflage. As he stepped out of the underbrush, Cassie saw it was Brad Keeler. The sun shone on his blond hair and glinted on the barrel of the gun he was carrying. He was staring down the hill at Cassie and the wolf.

One deep snarl after another came from Tokie's throat, a snarl that chilled Cassie to the bone. She thought, Tokie's trying to protect me. If only I had gotten him in the house first.

Brad began walking stealthily down the hill toward Cassie and the wolf, holding the rifle in readiness. Tokie retreated a step, taking Cassie with him, then took another step backwards, and another. His whole body was tense as Brad drew closer, and his snarls grew louder and more ominous.

When Cassie was sure Brad could hear her, she called out, "Don't come any closer! I can't hold him if you do."

"Get out of the way!" shouted Brad in return. "I can drop him before he gets across the yard. I'll shoot that wolf before he kills anyone."

"Don't you *dare* shoot him! Wolves are a protected species. And it's against the law to shoot a gun where people live. Besides, this wolf is my friend. He won't hurt anyone."

"You just don't want me to be a hero. The police are going to nail him anyway. He's a danger to the public."

"No he's not. He's my friend." She knelt down in front of Tokie, hanging on to him as best she could, her back to Brad. She said over her shoulder, "You'll have to shoot me first."

"Don't be stupid!" said Brad. Cassie saw Brad lower his gun and run one hand over his forehead.

Cassie yelled, "You're the one who's stupid! You're not allowed to shoot wolves. Besides, this one is my friend. The police will report you to Fish and Game and you'll get a citation. You'll have to pay a big fine, and they'll probably take away your hunting license, and you'll never get it back. Not ever! Put down your gun and back off. Now!"

She closed her eyes with her back to Brad, bracing herself for the shot and praying like crazy that he wouldn't shoot.

CHAPTER
23

"PUT DOWN THAT GUN," yelled Brad suddenly.

The gunshot was ten times louder than she expected, and it echoed back and forth over the hills. Cassie didn't feel a thing. Her eyes flew open, and she saw Brad lowering his smoking rifle after firing it up in the air. Not far away stood a man in uniform with an astonished look on his face. He held a rifle in readiness to shoot.

"Don't shoot that wolf!" Brad yelled at the man. "It's not wild, and it belongs to that girl!"

"Throw your gun down," said the man to Brad. "You'd better come with me. You'll have to explain this to the sheriff." He motioned to Brad with his rifle. "I'll take care of that wolf later. Come on!"

Brad hesitated but put his rifle on the ground. He turned at last and walked down the driveway, followed by the officer. Cassie was still shaking. The man said he would "take care of the wolf later." She knew what that meant. She had to get Tokie inside to keep him safe. No one would listen to her. No one would understand that Tokie wasn't dangerous. Everyone would want to shoot him. She had to protect him until she could find the owners.

She stood up, dug the fingers of both hands into Tokie's ruff, and dragged him step-by-step to the stairs leading to the back porch. She pulled him up the stairs and through the door propped open by the work shoes. She kicked away the shoes. The door swung shut.

"Whew!" exclaimed Cassie. She let go of Tokie's ruff and stood up. Tokie looked up uneasily at Cassie and then at the door. He put his nose to the crack under the door and sniffed deeply. He began digging at the floor, his nails gouging the wood.

"I'm sorry, but I have to keep you here," said Cassie. "It's to save your life. Remember the fun you had in here?"

She went into her bedroom, picked up the man-gled argyle sock that Tokie had liked so well, and re-turned to the kitchen. Tokie was still digging away at the door.

Cassie waved the sock at him, and the wolf looked up from his digging. Cassie wadded up the sock and threw it across the kitchen as far as she could. Tokie leaped to grab it, and Cassie quickly bolted the door. Tokie, the sock dangling from his mouth, looked with alarm at Cassie. He dropped the sock and re-turned to the door. His digging became frantic.

"You can't dig yourself out," Cassie told him, keep-ing her voice steady.

Tokie finally gave up at the back door and began trotting through the house, sniffing and scratching at every crack where there was a breath of fresh air—

underneath the front door and at the bottom and sides of the windows. He became more and more excited as he found no way out. He pushed aside furniture and knocked over a chair and the reading lamp with a crash. At the noise he leaped behind the sofa and peered out from behind it. Cassie would have laughed if she hadn't felt like crying.

Tokie studied the chair lying on its side and decided it looked threatening. He crouched and sprang, fastening his teeth around one of the chair legs. Cassie heard the crunch of wood. He shook it, and the leg broke off. Tokie trotted around the room with the piece of chair leg in his mouth.

Cassie watched the destruction silently. She thought, I'll have to work for years to pay for the damage. She couldn't put a stop to it, but she was past caring what happened to the house. She had to save her wolf.

Sally would help her, if she only knew. Sally certainly didn't want the wolf to be shot. Cassie tried to remember what she had done with Sally's business card. If she phoned animal control, they could radio to Sally in her truck. The card was in her room, somewhere.

A car went past slowly with a bullhorn blaring.

"Attention! Attention! There's a white wolf loose in this neighborhood. Please stay indoors with your doors and windows shut. We have him surrounded and will catch him very soon. I repeat, there's a white wolf loose . . ."

Cassie listened. She could hear Brad's voice in the background, over the bullhorn. He was trying to talk to the policeman.

The car with the bullhorn turned around, came back, and drew up in front of her house.

"Listen young lady," boomed the raspy voice. "We have everything under control; don't be afraid. Your house is completely surrounded. You can open the door to let the wolf out, and we'll catch him before he hurts anyone."

Cassie drew in her breath. She knew they didn't mean to catch him. They meant to shoot him.

Cassie frantically looked through the papers on her desk. At the bottom of the pile, she found Sally's card. She took the card with the number of animal control back to the telephone, and as she reached for the telephone, it rang, and Cassie jumped.

She picked up the receiver and answered it, keeping her eyes on Tokie. He moved closer to Cassie and cocked his head to one side, his golden eyes gleaming as he watched Cassie speaking into the phone.

A man's voice said, "This is Dr. Wesley of Cal State in Delgado Valley. My wife and I are wolf breeders, and we're still missing an Arctic wolf that escaped during the floods. We heard on the news that a white dog was seen in your area, and they believe he's a wolf. The TV camera showed your house number, and we traced you through the police. Do you know anything about our wolf?"

Cassie's legs shook. The owners! But Delgado

Valley? Why, that was miles and miles from here. She had known a wolf could travel really fast and far, but she was amazed that he had come all that way without getting caught or shot.

"Yes, I do," she said. "Actually, the wolf is locked up inside my house with me right now because someone up on the hill was shooting at him."

"Thank heavens you've got him safe. Mrs. Wesley and I will leave right away to come and get him. We're driving a white pickup truck with a big cage for wolves in the back. We'll pull up on your driveway, and when you see us, unlock the back door and we'll come in."

They told her how long it would take them to get there and gave her a phone number for their phone in the truck. "Call us if you have any trouble before we get there. And call the police and tell them the owners are on their way. Then they'll leave you alone, and the wolf will be safe."

As she put the receiver back, Tokie crouched and sprang on it, grabbing it in his strong jaws. Cassie smothered a shriek as Tokie shook it and shook it, then leaped away with the handset, ripping loose the telephone cord. He flung the handset over his shoulder and pounced upon the phone base. The plastic crackled and splintered. He ambushed it and killed it again and again until he was sure it was dead, and then he flung it away. He leered at Cassie and looked pleased with himself. He paced around the room.

There goes any chance of calling animal control, thought Cassie. Now what? She hoped nothing awful would happen before the wolf's owners arrived. She couldn't call the police, either, and tell them everything was okay. She thought of opening a window and calling to the police, but Tokie might try to jump out the window. He was too strong for her to keep him back. Who knew what he might try next? Even so, the police probably wouldn't believe her either. What could she do?

She went into her bedroom and plopped down cross-legged on her bed. Her heart raced. Tokie followed her into the bedroom and paced back and forth. After several long sniffs at the bottom of the window, he scratched at the windowsill. His toenails caught in one of the blue curtains that her father had hung for her. With a long tearing sound, half of the curtain came down and draped itself over Tokie. He loved the sound of tearing cloth. He put one paw on the curtain and began ripping it into shreds. Satisfied at last, he turned his head and peered at her, one golden eye shining from beneath the blue curtain rags. He shook himself free.

Cassie shivered. She patted a place beside her on the bed. "Oh come on, Tokie," she said. "Here's even another sock for you." She waved the mate of her argyle sock.

Tokie leaped onto the bed, almost knocking her over. He grabbed the sock and leaped down again to continue his pacing, the sock dangling from his mouth. Cassie gave up. She went into the living room and sat down in the brown chair.

"It's going to be okay, Tokie," Cassie said firmly, hoping the tone of her voice would reassure him. "Your owners are on their way here."

The filmy curtains at the front window moved as Tokie went by. In one bound he turned and attacked them, scratching until he pulled them all loose. They floated out into the room, one of them draping itself over Cassie and the brown chair. She pulled them away and dropped them on the floor.

The drapes on either side of the window moved slightly as she disposed of the curtains. Tokie made a dive for the drapes. He attacked them fiercely as if they were fighting back. He anchored them with his paws and ripped them apart with his great white teeth. He shook some of the pieces back and forth as though they were rabbits. He looked silly, but Cassie didn't smile. She got up and stared out the front window. Tokie stopped attacking the drapes and stood up at the window beside her, his front paws on the window sill.

A number of police and sheriff cars were lined up at the curb. Most of the uniformed men held guns. Cassie shivered. She saw a few people emerge from neighboring houses and gather at a safe distance behind the line of men in uniform.

"Young lady," the bullhorn rasped. "Open the door to let the wolf out so we can catch him before he attacks you."

Cassie drew in her breath. They meant to shoot him. She would have to explain to them that Tokie was her friend and that his owners were coming to get him, but they couldn't hear her from inside the house.

After watching Tokie, there was no way she was going to open a window. He wanted out too badly. Maybe she could try to yell out the door. After all, it had a safety chain. Tokie couldn't shove it open.

She made sure the safety chain on the front door was in place and opened the door the four inches the chain allowed. Instantly Tokie pushed her aside and shoved his head into the opening, sniffing deeply at the fresh air. He tried to force the door open wider and scratched at the doorjamb. Cassie put herself in front of him and tried to shove him back. He scratched at her leg and snarled.

"Stop that," pleaded Cassie, knowing it would only prove to the police that she was in danger. The scratch hurt, and she looked at the back of her leg. His nails had torn her jeans and drawn blood. He hadn't meant to hurt her, but she didn't think anyone would believe that.

Through the crack she watched a policeman walk from one patrol car to another, stop, and lean through the window, talking to the driver. When he turned to look at the house, Cassie called out through the crack, "I'm okay, and so is the wolf. He's not hurting anybody. Go away and leave us alone."

She heard a surprised murmur run through the

crowd. The bullhorn crackled and the raspy voice of the police captain boomed out. "Young lady, open the front door and let the wolf out before he attacks you."

"No," said Cassie loudly. "The wolf is my friend, and he won't attack me. He is going to stay here with me. Now go away and leave us alone. His owners are on their way here."

She began squeezing the door shut, and little by little Tokie retreated. At last he pulled his head out to look up at her, and she closed the door all the way.

She heaved a sigh of relief.

The bullhorn reached her even through the closed windows and doors. She was used to the raspy voice of the police captain on the bullhorn, but now a different voice reached her. It was familiar.

"You've got to leave her alone," said the voice. With a shock she realized it was Joe. *Joe?* What was he doing here?

There was more arguing, and the police captain's voice again came over the bullhorn. "Listen to me, Cassie," said the police captain. Joe must have told him her name. "Take the safety chain off the door and just stay quiet. If you need help, try to wave something at the window."

She wasn't going to take off the safety chain and give anyone a chance to come into the house. Tokie would get hurt for sure. She returned to the front door and called out Joe's name through the crack.

Joe walked out in front of the crowd, and she

motioned for him to come closer. Tokie stopped trying to get through the crack. He gave one soft "Woof!" and retreated behind Cassie.

Joe took several more steps forward and stopped.

C H A P T E R
24

"Listen, Joe," she said in a loud voice. "The owners of the wolf phoned me, and they are on their way here to pick him up. They'll be here in a couple of hours. Try to make the police and the crowds get away from the house. They are upsetting the wolf."

"Right!" he said. He grinned. "Man oh man, that's some Eskimo dog you've got there!" She saw him start talking to the police captain.

Cassie moved the brown chair so she could look out the front windows while she waited. The captain called the policemen to his squad car and gestured at the crowd. The men talked to the people, and soon the crowd began to disperse. The TV news van stayed at the curb. Cassie settled down and talked reassuringly to Tokie, who occasionally stopped pacing to lean against her knees, whining and squeaking.

A few more neighbors came out of their houses, taking shelter on their porches or behind hedges. Suddenly Cassie saw her mother, still in her waitress uniform, hurrying past the cordon of cars to the man with the bullhorn. Striding briskly along beside her in a business suit was a tall, good-looking man with silvery white hair.

Cassie knew the people her mother worked with, and she had never seen this man before. It had to be her mother's friend, Fred What's-his-name.

"Cassie!" exclaimed her mother's voice, amplified a hundred times by the bullhorn. "Are you all right? Is that really a wolf in there with you? Can't you run out the back door while he's in the living room?"

Cassie sighed and opened the front door again as far as the chain would allow. Tokie shoved his head into the crack, sniffing at the open air. Cassie put her knee against his head, but this time he didn't scratch.

"I'm okay, Mom. The wolf is my friend. We'll be all right if everybody will just go away and leave us alone." She looked at the people still there and thought, Yeah, right.

Her mother went on, "I've been so scared ever since they told me at work they heard on the radio about a wolf being seen in the neighborhood where we live, and then they said he was in somebody's house, and then *on TV they showed our house.* The manager let me off from work right away. Cassie, how *could* you *do* such a thing?"

Cassie thought a minute. "Well, he was hungry, and he came in our backyard, so I fed him. I thought he was an Eskimo dog."

A murmur ran through the crowd. Some people laughed.

Her mother spoke again on the bullhorn. "Mr. Schirmeyer heard about the wolf on the news, too, so he came over to see if he could help. Is there anything he could do for you?"

Cassie thought, he could go away and leave you alone. And you could stop going out with him.

Out loud she said, "No, there's nothing you can do right now. The owners will be here in a couple of hours to pick up the wolf. We just have to wait."

Tokie had given up pacing and trying to get through the front door. He went back to the sofa, jumped up, and went to work again excavating his hole in the middle cushion.

"Oh no!" shrieked Cassie. Then she realized someone might think she was being attacked. She looked at the sofa and groaned. It was beyond repair anyhow. Tokie was making it into a den. She picked up one of the wolf books and sat down in the brown chair. She had to do something to take her mind off the disaster. At first it was hard to concentrate, but little by little she was carried away by the words.

In a wolf pack, the adults play for hours with the cubs, she read. They are extremely tolerant and affectionate, but they're not overpermissive. They educate the cubs very carefully. Maybe Tokie had a family. She could see him taking loving care of his pups, teaching them how to hunt, and playing tricks on the older wolves. She smiled to herself. She read on for what seemed like hours until the bullhorn startled her.

"Everyone move back and let the truck pull into the driveway," said the police captain's voice. "Move back, everybody. *All* the way back."

Tokie had been curled up in his den in the middle of the sofa while she had been reading. He lifted his head from his den, clouds of foam filling all around him. He cocked his head to one side, listening.

Cassie heard a truck go up the driveway and stop in front of the garage. She hurried to the back door, unlocked it, and went back to get Tokie. The wolf jumped down, shook off the foam filling, and trotted to the side windows to look out, but he couldn't see the driveway from there. The back door opened and closed, and a woman's voice called, "Quasar!"

Cassie waited to see what Tokie would do. Would he recognize his owners? Would he want to leave her? Tokie's tail began to wave slowly. He went cautiously toward the kitchen and peered around the door. He suddenly disappeared into the kitchen. Cassie sighed. Tokie knew. She heard the voices of a man and a woman exclaiming over Tokie, though they were calling him Quasar.

The woman was laughing as they came into the living room, Tokie racing in circles for joy and jumping up on them, swinging his tail back and forth furiously. The woman wore blue jeans and a plaid shirt that had already been mauled by Tokie's enthusiastic welcome, but she pushed a lock of shiny brown hair out of her eyes and smiled.

"So you're Cassie," she said. "We are *very* glad to meet you."

The man held out one hand to Cassie as though she were a grown-up. Cassie shook it. He looked very distinguished with his full beard and horn-rimmed glasses. What a time to have company, she thought, when their house couldn't have looked worse.

The man said, "I'm Robert Wesley, and this is my wife, Gloria. Young lady, we owe you a great deal of thanks for saving our wolf."

"We certainly do," said Mrs. Wesley, bracing herself against Tokie's leaps and kisses. She had a difficult time keeping her balance. She finally gave up,

laughing, and sank cross-legged onto the floor. Tokie immediately jumped into her lap, almost knocking her over. With huge paws on her shoulders, he slobbered over her face. She kept laughing and trying to turn her face away. He suddenly grabbed her left leg in his huge jaws and pretended to shake it as though he would tear it off.

While he was attacking her in mock fury, she pulled out of her jeans' pocket a chain leash and made a loop in one end. She hugged him hard. When he let go of her leg she slipped the loop over his head. He leaned against her, squeaking and whining deep in his throat.

Cassie watched them, feeling jealous, when a strange new feeling of pride came over her. All by herself she had saved Tokie. She, Cassie, had protected him from the police, from the sheriff's posse, and from Brad Keeler. She smiled and straightened up. "I'm sorry the place is such a mess. . . ."

"Gracious!" exclaimed Mrs. Wesley, looking around for the first time. "I'll bet Quasar did this when he discovered he couldn't get out!"

"Yeah, he got pretty excited." She perched on the arm of the sofa. "I didn't care about the house as long as Tokie was safe."

Mrs. Wesley said, "It's a good thing for Tokie and for us that you felt that way."

"Don't worry about the house," said Dr. Wesley. "We'll pay for all the damages. We're just happy to have Quasar back safe and sound. He's one of Gloria's favorites."

Cassie sighed. "It's a good thing he's going home with you. I couldn't figure out how I was going to get out of this mess."

"I believe it," said Mrs. Wesley. "You are a very sensitive girl to make friends with a wolf and a brave girl to do all the things you did to save him. We had just about given up hope of ever finding him alive."

Dr. Wesley smiled at Cassie. "Now that you've taken care of our wolf for a while, how would you like to have a wolf of your own?"

CHAPTER
25

Cassie was silent for a minute. She smiled and shook her head. "Absolutely not. I wouldn't *want* one. Wolves are not pets—they are wild animals. Look what happened when I was just trying to take *care* of one."

They laughed. Dr. Wesley said, "I wanted to hear you say that. A lot of people think it would be great to have a wolf as a pet."

"Would they be in for a big surprise! A wolf can't ever be a pet! But wolves sure are interesting. I want to learn a lot more about them. The trouble is, the more I learn, the less I seem to know what they're really like."

"You're very perceptive," said Dr. Wesley. "Trying to draw conclusions about a wolf is like shoveling smoke."

Cassie nodded. "Yeah, I never thought of that."

Mrs. Wesley asked, "How did you meet and make friends with Quasar?"

"Well . . . ," said Cassie, brightening. While she talked, the wolf paced back and forth as far as his chain would allow. From time to time he climbed into Mrs. Wesley's lap and licked and nuzzled her. Once he jumped up on the sofa beside Cassie, swinging his tail, and smeared his tongue over her face.

"I see he's very fond of you," said Mrs. Wesley.

Cassie hugged him and finished her story. "But I want to know why you have wolves. What kind of work do you do?"

"I teach wildlife biology at Cal State in Delgado Valley, and my specialty is wolves. I'm what you call an ethologist," said Dr. Wesley.

"What's that?"

"Someone who studies animal behavior in their natural habitat."

"But you said your wolves are in a compound, and a compound isn't a natural habitat."

He nodded. "It's a pretty big compound, twenty acres or so, but you're right. A group of us goes up to Alaska and northern Canada every year, and we live with the Inuit for several months at a time. That's when we study wolves in the wild."

"Wow! That sounds great!" exclaimed Cassie.

"We're raising our wolves to be ambassadors."

"Ambassadors!" exclaimed Cassie.

Mrs. Wesley laughed. "Ambassadors of education, for schools and for service clubs like Rotary."

She went on, "Few people know what wolves are really like, so we try to teach people."

Dr. Wesley said, "Wolves have had a terrible reputation, beginning with the first European immigrants who came to America.

"They brought with them their medieval myths and legends about wolves. They believed that the wolf was pure evil, Satan personified.

"As the pioneers moved West, the myths and

legends moved with them, spreading terror and fear of wolves among the settlers. Eventually their goal became the extermination of the wolf. That was a big mistake, because the wolf as a predator helped shape the herds of deer and elk and caribou to keep them strong and fast, and to prevent overgrazing of grasslands."

Dr. Wesley said, "We find that educating school children is a good way to bring about change in public attitude."

Mrs. Wesley's eyes sparkled. "When I talk to a classroom of children about wolves, I like to ask them to draw a picture of a wolf before I bring in the ambassador wolf. Usually their pictures show the wolf as a frightening thing to see, and the wolf's teeth are the biggest thing in the picture.

"After they've met the wolf, I ask them to draw another picture of the wolf."

Dr. Wesley said, "And guess what the new pictures show."

"I don't know," said Cassie.

"The wolf is an ordinary animal, more like a dog, and the biggest thing about him is his feet!" said Mrs. Wesley.

They all laughed.

Cassie said, "I'd give anything to do work like that. I've always wanted to work with animals, but I knew I didn't want to be a vet."

"You certainly would enjoy this kind of work. In college, you should major in biology and then concentrate in a special field, such as animal behavior."

"Cool!" exclaimed Cassie. "I didn't know there were real jobs like that. But college costs an awful lot."

"You'll get there if you're determined to," Dr. Wesley said. "If you work hard and show people you're serious, you can. And there are scholarships available for young people with special talents or abilities."

Mrs. Wesley said, "Why don't you visit us for a month or so next summer when school is out? You can see the compound and meet all our wolves." She ruffled the wolf's fur as he leaned against her knees. "If you're not afraid of hard work, there's plenty to do, like cleaning kennels and preparing the food for the wolves."

"I can *work* for you?"

"If your mother will let you. Of course you'll be paid. There'll even be a spring litter of wolf pups to feed and look after."

Cassie felt giddy with joy. Her future without Toklata had been bleak, but suddenly it was blindingly bright. "You bet! Of *course* I'll come. That would be really cool."

"You'll see Quasar again and meet his pups."

"I'd *love* cuddling the wolf pups, if the mother wolf would let me."

"She won't have anything to say about it. The pups are taken from the mother when they're only a couple of days old and are brought up by humans. They have to be bottle-fed."

"Oh, the poor things! Why?"

"If the mother wolf brings them up, they could

never be handled by humans at all; they would always be completely wild. It's a lot of work for a person to bring up wolf pups. The pups have to be fed every couple of hours. You would be a big help. A pup has to be socialized so humans can handle him when he's full grown."

"I'll do it! I'll do it! I *know* my mother will let me."

After a while the Wesleys said they had to leave; they had a long drive home. Mrs. Wesley stood up and tugged lightly on the chain, and Quasar moved restlessly beside her.

It was time to say good-bye. Cassie remembered Mrs. Ulmer saying she let Mr. Ulmer take her dog to the vet to be put to sleep because she couldn't bear to say good-bye. Maybe that's why Cassie's father left without saying good-bye to her, she thought. Maybe he figured that if he had said good-bye, he might not have been able to leave. Maybe, she repeated to herself. Just maybe.

Now she had to say good-bye to Toklata.

She would try to be strong. She took a deep breath, knelt on the floor, and buried her face in the familiar, coarse fur. She hugged him tight for a moment before he wriggled out of her grasp. Then he turned around and gave her face a slobbering kiss with his tongue.

Cassie could feel the tears welling up in her eyes.

"Be good, Toklata," she choked.

Mrs. Wesley put her arms around Cassie and hugged her. "You'll hear from us soon, and I'll talk to your mother. I'll ask her to get in touch with a house cleaning service and a furniture store, and we'll pay the bill. Tell your mother not to worry. And we'll see you next summer."

They led Toklata out through the kitchen while Cassie stood in the middle of the living room and told herself, Don't cry, do not cry. Then she went to the window and waved good-bye as the truck drove away. She could see Tokie in the back, frisking happily.

She wiped her face, unchained the front door, and went out. There was a cheer from the crowd, and her mother rushed forward to throw both arms around her.

"Honey, I was so scared for you."

"I'm okay. Really." Cassie hugged her mother back and then saw the man in the business suit right behind them. She stiffened as she remembered her resolve. Now was her chance to say, "Oh Mom, Dad phoned this afternoon, and he's coming home. I'm sure he'll want to meet your friend from Ventura." She would figure out later how to explain her actions to her mother. Nearby was the police captain talking into the bullhorn, telling the crowd to disperse. It occurred to Cassie that if she talked to her mother near the bullhorn, everybody would know. The bullhorn would be perfect. She edged toward the captain.

Cassie's mother said in a happy voice, "Cassie, I have some wonderful news for you."

C H A P T E R
26

"Wonderful news? I bet," said Cassie. And then the vision of the white wolf flashed before her eyes. She thought, If we were wolves, I wouldn't try to change her or the way she feels about her friend. I would let her be herself, and I would love her just the way she is.

Cassie took a big breath and smiled up at her mother. Then she noticed a gray-haired woman standing beside the man.

Her mother smiled happily and motioned to the couple. "I want you to meet Mr. and Mrs. Schirmeyer, my new bosses. They're opening a new restaurant here in town next month, another Spinning Wheel, and I'm going to be the manager and the one in charge of personnel."

Cassie froze.

Mr. Schirmeyer smiled. "We're lucky to have your mother help us get started. She's very talented in dealing with people."

Mrs. Schirmeyer gestured to the dispersing crowd and said, "This has been rather exciting. You seem to have inherited your mother's ability to handle unusual situations."

"Your bosses? Another Spinning Wheel?" said Cassie, her mind blank. She was in a daze.

Cassie's mother said, "Remember, we drove to Ventura to have dinner in the restaurant there? The Spinning Wheel? I met Mrs. Schirmeyer, and they showed me around the whole place. The one here in town is going to be just like the one in Ventura once it's finished. I'll love working there."

Cassie blinked. "Why didn't you tell me this before?"

"I didn't want to say anything and get your hopes up until I signed the contract. But it's for sure, now."

Cassie's knees felt weak. "Oh." She looked at her mother's glowing face. "Gee, Mom, I'm really glad for you."

"Let's go in the house, and we'll tell you all about it."

Cassie's mind began to work again. "Listen, Mom, I've got to warn you before you go in. Things are really a mess. The wolf sort of went crazy when he was shut in the house. But Dr. and Mrs. Wesley said they would pay for everything, and you're not to worry."

She stood aside and let them enter. Her mother shrieked, and Mr. Schirmeyer said, "Great Scot!" Cassie heard Mrs. Schirmeyer say "Oh mercy me!" in a faint voice.

It suddenly hit Cassie that Mr. Schirmeyer wasn't dating her mother after all, and that her mother had a great new job. And Cassie had almost blown it.

189

"Whew," said Cassie, and she followed them in.

Cassie wanted to sleep in on Sunday, but it didn't work out that way. When her mother was ready for work, she told Cassie, "I still don't know how you could take care of a wolf all that time and not get hurt. And to think that you've been working at the neighbors' to pay for his food. I didn't know you wanted a dog that much."

Cassie smiled. "Mom, don't forget to report that our phone is out of order. But don't tell them a wolf chewed it up. They won't believe you."

"Oh, I think they will. Honey, you're front-page news. You should see the people outside waiting to talk to you."

Cassie sat up in bed and started to laugh. "Yeah, but were they scared to come near when Toklata was here in the house."

"I know. We all were. Cassie, if you want a dog that badly, I guess you've earned the right to have one. We can go down to the pound next week, and you can choose the one you want."

Cassie shook her head. "Thanks, Mom, but I don't want a dog right now. It's not a good idea. You've got a job, and you're away most of the time. And I'll be in school. It's not fair to a dog to have to be shut up in the house all day."

"Even if we get the backyard fenced in? I think we'll be able to afford fencing with my new job."

"Mom, that's nice, but I don't want a dog until I can spend a lot of time with him and work with him and train him really well. Besides, I want to go down to the Wesleys' house next summer in Delgado Valley and work for them like I told you. I wouldn't want to leave my dog for that long a time."

Cassie sighed. "Someday I'll have a dog, but not yet."

"What will you do with that big sack of dog kibble you worked so hard for?"

"I guess I'll give it to Joe Pinatelli for his dog, Skunk."

Her mother leaned over and kissed Cassie.

"Cassie, I want you to know how proud of you I am. You took care of a real wolf and saved him from getting shot, even though you had half the sheriff's department down on you. Everyone is talking about how brave you were."

"I wasn't brave. I was really scared to death."

They both laughed.

While her mother was at work, Cassie planned to do her homework and read more about wolves. She was thankful she had a lot to do so she wouldn't think so much about Tokie. But first she wanted to apologize to Karen Kimura for being so rude— dashing off like that yesterday with no explanation.

When Cassie dressed, she was surprised that the gardening had stretched her clothes so much. Her jeans were almost loose. She put an old leather belt through the loops and pulled it up tight.

She walked down the street to Karen Kimura's house.

Karen opened the door, and her dark eyes

sparkled when she saw who it was. "Cassie! Come on in! I couldn't imagine why you left in such a hurry. No wonder! I never would have guessed you were friends with a *real wolf.* You are one brave girl."

"I didn't mean to be rude," said Cassie, "but I was really scared he would get shot. And you were about to tell me something."

"Yes, I was. I have a surprise for you."

"I remember."

"You told me your math class at John Fremont School had only four computers, isn't that right?"

"Yes, but the school can't afford any more."

"I talked to the head of our public relations department. To promote our company, they are going to donate four more computers to your school, especially for your math class."

Cassie gasped. "That's fantastic! The teachers and the kids will love it!"

"After the publicity of your wolf story, the company will be even happier to give your school four computers."

"I bet I get a turn to use one more often, too," said Cassie, grinning.

She stopped smiling when she looked through Karen Kimura's window up at the hill behind her house. She remembered how frightened she had been when Brad Keeler had come down the hill with his rifle. She was glad that Brad had taken his rifle and gone home after their confrontation. He'd be mad at her for a while, she thought, but he'd get over it, especially when he found out he really *would* have lost his hunting license just as she told him. She'd never tell anyone that he was really going to shoot the wolf.

Cassie sighed. People definitely needed to know what wolves were *really* like.

Maybe she should give an oral report on wolves for her science class. Then she remembered the rows of unfriendly faces and how her tongue stuck to the roof of her mouth. Her heart began to pound at the thought of standing up in front of the class.

She took a deep breath. She would just do it, anyway. She had to. No, she *wanted* to.

She was sure Mr. Crowell would say yes. She could hardly wait.

Frances Wilbur was born in Mankato, Minnesota. In 1942 she graduated from Beloit College with a B.A. in English literature, and ten days after graduation she reported to the Signal Intelligence Service in Washington, D.C., where she spent the war years working as a cryptanalyst. After the war Wilbur lived in Spain and in Italy, where her children played "Normans and Saracens" rather than cowboys and Indians. Since settling in California, Wilbur has worked as a newspaper columnist and, for twenty years, as a director of a summer horsemanship camp. She is married and is the mother of five grown children. *The Dog with Golden Eyes* is her third book.

Interior design by Will Powers
Typeset in Amerigo BT
by Stanton Publication Services, Inc.
Printed on acid-free 55# Sebago Antique Cream paper
by Maple-Vail Book Manufacturing Group

If you enjoyed this book, you will also want to read these other Milkweed novels:

Gildaen, The Heroic Adventures of a Most Unusual Rabbit *by Emilie Buchwald*

Chicago Tribune *Book Festival Award, Best Book for Ages 9–12*

Gildaen is befriended by a mysterious being who has lost his memory but not the ability to change shape at will. Together they accept the perilous task of thwarting the evil sorcerer, Grimald, in this tale of magic, villainy, and heroism.

The Gumma Wars *by David Haynes*

Larry "Lu" Underwood and his fellow West 7th Wildcats have been looking forward to Tony Rodriguez's birthday fiesta all year—only to discover that Lu must also spend the day with his two feuding "gummas," the name he gave his grandmothers when he was just learning to talk. The two "gummas," Gumma Jackson and Gumma Underwood, are hostile to one another, especially when it comes to claiming the affection of their only grandson. On the action-packed day of Tony's birthday, Lu, a friend, and the gummas find themselves exploring the sights of Minneapolis and St. Paul—and eventually find themselves enjoying each other's company.

Business As Usual *by David Haynes*

In Mr. Harrison's sixth-grade class, the West 7th Wildcats must learn how to run a business. Kevin

Olsen, one of the Wildcats as well as the class clown, is forced out of the Wildcat group and into an unwilling alliance working in a group with the Wildcats' nemesis, Jenny Pederson. In the process of making staggering amounts of cookies for Marketplace Day, the classmates venture into the realm of free enterprise, discovering more than they imagined about business, the world, and themselves.

The Monkey Thief *by Aileen Kilgore Henderson*

New York Public Library Best Books of the Year: "Books for the Teen Age"

Steve Hanson doesn't normally lead an exciting life. But when he's sent to the Costa Rican rain forest to help his uncle set up a nature preserve, Steve discovers a world totally unlike anything he could see from the cushions of his couch back home—a world filled with giant trees and insects, mysterious sounds, and the constant companionship of monkeys swinging in the branches overhead. When Steve crosses paths with a dangerous *huaquero,* or treasure hunter, it takes all of his new survival skills and the help of his new friends to get him out safely.

The Summer of the Bonepile Monster
by Aileen Kilgore Henderson

Milkweed Prize for Children's Literature
Alabama Library Association 1996 Juvenile/
Young Adult Award

Eleven-year-old Hollis Orr has been sent to spend the summer with Grancy, his father's grandmother, in rural Dolliver, Alabama, while his parents "work things out."

As summer begins, Hollis encounters a road called Bonepile Hollow, barred by a gate and a real skull and bones mounted on a board. "Things that go down that road don't ever come back," he is told. Thus begins the mystery that plunges Hollis into real danger.

I Am Lavina Cumming *by Susan Lowell*

Mountains & Plains Booksellers Association Award

In 1905, ten-year-old Lavina is sent from her home on the Bosque Ranch in Arizona Territory to live with her aunt in the city of Santa Cruz, California. Armed with the Cumming family motto, "Courage," Lavina deals with a new school, homesickness, a very spoiled cousin, an earthquake, and a big decision about her future.

The Boy with Paper Wings *by Susan Lowell*

Confined to bed with a viral fever, eleven-year-old Paul sails a paper airplane into his closet and propels himself into mysterious and dangerous realms in this exciting and fantastical adventure. Paul finds himself trapped in the military diorama on his closet floor, out to stop the evil commander, KRON. Armed only with paper and the knowledge of how to fold it, Paul uses his imagination and courage to find his way out of dilemmas and disasters.

The Secret of the Ruby Ring *by Yvonne MacGrory*

Winner of Ireland's Bisto "Book of the Year" Award

Lucy gets a very special birthday present, a star ruby ring, from her grandmother and finds herself transported to Langley Castle in the Ireland of 1885. At first,

she is intrigued by castle life, in which she is the low-
liest servant, until she loses the ruby ring and her only
way home.

A Bride for Anna's Papa *by Isabel R. Marvin*

Milkweed Prize for Children's Literature

Life on Minnesota's iron range in 1907 is not easy for
thirteen-year-old Anna Kallio. Her mother's death has
left Anna to take care of the house, her young brother,
and her father, a blacksmith in the dangerous iron
mines. So she and her brother plot to find their father
a new wife, even attempting to arrange a match with
one of the "mail order" brides arriving from Finland.

Minnie *by Annie M. G. Schmidt*

*Winner of the Netherlands' Silver Pencil Prize as
One of the Best Books of the Year*

Miss Minnie is a cat. Or rather, she *was* a cat. She is
now a human, and she's not at all happy to be one. As
Minnie tries to find and reverse the cause of her trans-
formation, she brings her reporter friend, Mr. Tibbs,
news from the cats' gossip hotline—including revealing
information that one of the town's most prominent
citizens is not the animal lover he appears to be.

Behind the Bedroom Wall *by Laura E. Williams*

Milkweed Prize for Children's Literature

It is 1942. Thirteen-year-old Korinna Rehme is an active
member of her local *Jungmädel,* a Nazi youth group,
along with many of her friends. Korinna's parents, how-

ever, secretly are members of an underground group providing a means of escape to the Jews of their city and are, in fact, hiding a refugee family behind the wall of Korinna's bedroom. As Korinna comes to know the family, and their young daughter, her sympathies begin to turn. But when someone tips off the Gestapo, loyalties are put to the test and Korinna must decide in what she believes and whom she trusts.

Milkweed Editions publishes with the intention of making a humane impact on society, in the belief that literature is a transformative art uniquely able to convey the essential experiences of the human heart and spirit.

To that end, Milkweed publishes distinctive voices of literary merit in handsomely designed, visually dynamic books, exploring the ethical, cultural, and esthetic issues that free societies need continually to address.

Milkweed Editions is a not-for-profit press.